*She turned to greet the visitor. Suddenly the very small galley felt even smaller. Deepti swallowed, craning her neck to look at the man.*

He was tall.

At five foot three, she knew most people were tall compared to her, but he was tall even on that basis—at a guess, a few inches over six foot. Thank goodness the ceilings in the yacht were incredibly high. Although he was wearing a polo shirt, it wasn't the standard crew uniform one, nor the kind that designated the people on the bridge. She definitely hadn't been introduced to this man earlier in the day. There was no way she would have forgotten him.

He was probably the most stunning man she'd ever seen in the flesh. She couldn't stop staring at the perfection of his features—a strong jaw; straight, almost arrogant nose; dark brown eyes that could stare deep into her soul. She licked her lips, her mouth suddenly dry.

He exuded power and control. This was obviously a man who was used to being in charge. And equally obviously, with his unblinking stare, someone who was not happy.

Dear Reader,

When I'm writing this, there is frost on the ground and the low sun is strong and bright—it's cold but beautiful. On days like this, I can't help but dream of sailing off into the sunset. My heroine, Deepti, gets to live out this dream when she sails from Southampton to Singapore on a superyacht.

Being at sea for days and exploring different countries when the yacht is docked is a unique experience for Deepti. And an unexpected added benefit is getting to know and spend time with handsome yacht owner Matteo. There is an obvious attraction and affection between them, but before they can truly explore their connection, they must learn to trust. Not only do they have to learn to trust each other, but they also need to learn to trust in themselves and believe they deserve true love.

I've loved joining Deepti and Matteo on their journey, and I hope you will too.

Much love,

*Ruby Basu*

# Sailing to Singapore with the Tycoon

**Ruby Basu**

—

Recycling programs
for this product may
not exist in your area.

ISBN-13: 978-1-335-59635-2

Sailing to Singapore with the Tycoon

Copyright © 2023 by Ruby Basu

For questions and comments about the quality of this book, please contact us at CustomerService@Harlequin.com.

Harlequin Enterprises ULC
22 Adelaide St. West, 41st Floor
Toronto, Ontario M5H 4E3, Canada
www.Harlequin.com

**Printed in U.S.A.**

**Ruby Basu** lives in the beautiful Chilterns with her husband, two children and the cutest dog in the world. She worked for many years as a lawyer and policy lead in the Civil Service. As the second of four children, Ruby connected strongly with *Little Women*'s Jo March and was scribbling down stories from a young age. She loves creating new characters and worlds.

### Also by Ruby Basu

### Harlequin Romance

*Baby Surprise for the Millionaire*
*Cinderella's Forbidden Prince*

Visit the Author Profile page
at Harlequin.com for more titles.

For my special assistant, Toffy, as promised.

# CHAPTER ONE

DEEPTI ROY PUT her suitcases in the cabin that would be her home for the next thirty days.

When her friend Alex had told her he would be head chef on a super-yacht that would be sailing from Southampton to Singapore, and suggested she should join him as a crew member, she'd jumped at the chance. Singapore had been top of her list of places to visit ever since she'd fallen in love with it when watching some of her favourite Asian dramas. But, more than that, she needed to get away from England— and running away to sea had sounded perfect.

With its twin beds with a small desk in between, enough storage, an *en suite* bathroom with a shower and even a tiny window, her cabin was more spacious and well-furnished than she'd originally imagined. But it was probably in line with what she should have expected after she'd toured the rest of the yacht.

When she'd been standing on the dock at

Southampton and caught her first view of *Serendipity*, she'd stood in open-mouthed awe. She imagined her response had been similar to how the passengers had felt when they'd first seen *Titanic*. She only hoped her voyage would have a better outcome—although, with how her life had been going recently, she should probably expect the worst. The only stroke of luck she'd had recently was the timing of the journey—she'd read March was one of the best times of year to visit Singapore.

No... Deepti deliberately turned her thoughts away from the direction they were headed. Although things had imploded spectacularly recently, she still had been given this opportunity to work with her friend. She suspected he'd called in significant favours to get everything sorted out for her to become crew at such short notice and she would be grateful for their friendship for ever. She wouldn't let him down.

As soon as she'd unpacked and freshened up, she would head to the galley to report for duty. She could just about remember where she was from Alex's tour of the yacht when she'd first got on board.

Even though she'd known they would be sailing in a top-of-the-line luxury yacht, Deepti had still been unprepared for its splendour. With five upper decks and one deck below the waterline,

*Serendipity* was almost as large as a cruise liner, with exquisite and expensive equipment, furnishings and décor, and top-of-the-range water toys for entertainment.

Alex hadn't shown her the very top deck because it belonged to the owner—she would probably never have a reason to go onto that deck. Below the owner's deck, the upper deck had been turned into a business suite with a board room, conference room and the owner's offices.

The main deck below that had the state rooms for the guests. She hadn't wanted to leave the stunning main salon with its full-height, sliding glass walls which opened on three sides. There were plush white sofas with accent cushions in blue and yellow on one end, next to an outside side deck with more seating and a bar. At the other end of the salon was a large twenty-seater dining table.

Alex had specifically pointed out a large mirror behind the dining table. He'd pressed a secret panel on the floor and the mirror had slid open to reveal a small galley. It was a secondary galley, mainly used for food service, but Alex had explained she would be based there primarily when she was making her desserts. Inside the galley was a small lift which took them directly to the lower deck, with the main galley and some crew quarters on one side.

On the other end of the yacht from the crew quarters there was effectively a beach club with an indoor swimming pool, steam room, sauna, rooms for beauty therapies and a gym, the ceiling of which was the underside view of a glass-bottomed outdoor swimming pool on the deck above.

She hadn't been to that deck, since Alex had explained it was for guests—Deepti would have no reason to go there.

Rather than take Deepti to the lowest deck, where there were more crew cabins, the laundry and storage, Alex had ended the tour on the deck above it so he could introduce her to some of the crew, and then he'd taken her to her cabin.

She quickly unpacked her belongings then made her way to the galley, luckily easy to find, since she knew it was on the same level. Alex was talking to the head steward. When Alex had introduced her to Deepti earlier, Deepti had noticed a closeness between the two of them.

Now, as she watched them interact, their body language and the way they looked at each other made it clear there was something romantic between them. It also explained why the head steward had agreed to the unusual sleeping situation, whereby Deepti effectively had a cabin to herself, whereas she would usually have had to share with the other assistant chef or a member of the steward crew.

When she left, Deepti raised an eyebrow and smirked. Alex smiled but didn't say anything, and Deepti didn't press. Alex had been through so many bad relationships and, although misery loved company, Deepti would much rather her friend was happy with a new romance than wallow with her in their tragic love lives.

Deepti's insides clenched, which was becoming an automatic response any time she thought about her ex-boyfriend. She needed to concentrate on looking forward. At some point, she would need to think about getting her career back on track and clearing her name but, for now, she was working as crew on a super-yacht and needed to give her current job one hundred per cent.

'We're going to get underway around twelve and my current instruction is to serve lunch at one p.m.,' Alex said. 'There will only be two for lunch in the main dining room—Mr Di Corrado and his assistant.'

'His assistant is eating with him rather than us?'

'It's a working lunch. The nanny will have lunch with us after she's fed the children, and then both will have dinner with crew.'

Deepti nodded. 'I see. So, the nanny eats with

us but the assistant eats with his boss.' Deepti didn't know whether that was an unusual arrangement, but the assistant and nanny were probably in a peculiar position on a yacht: not a crew member but not exactly treated as a guest either. It almost felt as if she were in a period drama, with the upstairs-downstairs division. This voyage was going to be a unique experience.

'So what do you need me to make for lunch?' she asked.

Alex referred to his notes. 'Mr Di Corrado hasn't requested dessert, and the crew will have fruit and yoghurt, so why don't you start thinking about what dessert you want to serve for dinner? There will be four for the main dining. No particular dietary requirements indicated.'

'Four.' Deepti furrowed her brow. 'How can there be four? You said it was only the owner and his assistant for lunch. What will the other guests be doing for lunch?'

Alex gave a belly laugh. 'The other guests will arrive by helicopter in the evening.'

Deepti rolled her eyes in an exaggerated manner. 'Of course—this yacht has a helipad. I should have guessed. The lifestyles of the rich and famous.'

'I would have thought you'd be used to this lifestyle.'

'Me? Definitely not. Not even my clients have this level of luxury.' Deepti's smile faltered. 'Ex-clients now, I guess.'

'Sorry, Dee. I shouldn't have said anything.' Alex's face fell, so she hastened to reassure him.

'No, don't apologise. I can't bury my head in the sand and pretend I didn't get fired.' She tried to give a nonchalant shrug but assumed, from Alex's sympathetic head tilt, she hadn't been suc-cessful.

'Have you had any more thoughts about what you're going to do about your work back home?' he asked.

She sighed. 'No idea. My head's been in a whirl, trying to decide what to do for the best. This op-portunity has come at the perfect time for me. You are my saviour.' She put her hand to her heart.

Alex grinned and playfully rubbed her head. 'Anything for you. Always. You know you're like a sister to me.'

'Ditto,' Deepti replied. 'Like a brother, that is. In all seriousness, thank you. I don't know what I would have done without you or Mum and Dad.'

'How did your parents react?'

'As expected, completely supportive. I went to stay with them for a few days to get away from London. Which is for the best,' she added with a laugh, 'Because I had to stop my mum marching into my boss's office and demanding justice for me.'

'That does sound like her.'

'I just hate letting them down.'

'Deepti, you didn't do anything wrong. Your mum's right—this is a complete injustice. Anyone who knows you can see that.'

Deepti clamped her lips together to hold in her emotions. After having had her integrity and honesty questioned by the people she'd worked closely with for seven years, all her working life, it meant so much to have the absolute confidence of Alex and her parents.

How had her life imploded so completely in such a short time? Only three weeks before, she'd been working on a proposal she'd expected would land a huge client and all but guarantee a promotion. Instead, she'd lost the deal and then, barely a day later, an existing client had switched to a competitor. She'd consequently lost her job mere days after her boyfriend of almost a year had broken up with her.

This opportunity to spend a month at sea was a lifeline before she sorted out what she was going to do in the future. If she had any hope of getting back into the financial sector, she needed to find out how the deal had gone so sour. And, if that wasn't possible, what could she do instead?

The loss of her career was a much more significant blow than her relationship ending. That hadn't come as such a shock. Although they'd been together for almost a year, it had never been a grand passion. For her, it had been about companionship rather than love. The only thing surprising about its end was the timing.

'I know my ex is involved somehow,' she said. 'It's too much of a coincidence for him not to be.' She waved her hands in front of her face, as if trying to brush away her thoughts. 'Anyway, I need to get some distance and clarity if I'm going to have any chance of sorting out what happened.'

'I always thought he was a creep,' Alex said.

'Really? You met him once about six months ago for two hours.'

Alex shrugged. 'I did tell you I thought you could do better.'

'You did, but you say that about most men I've dated.'

'And I've been right so far.'

'Perhaps I'm just a terrible judge of character,' she said, not sure she was joking.

'You can't be that bad, Dee. You chose me as one of your best friends.'

'True,' Deepti replied with a grin. She could always rely on Alex to raise her spirits. She reached out and covered his hand for a brief moment. 'Thank you, Alex. You're always looking out for me.'

'Always will. You know there's Internet access onboard if you need it? There's a sign-up sheet in the crew lounge.'

'I guess I will have to brush up my CV.'

'What will you do if you get interviews?'

'Cross my fingers they'll do them by video. If worse comes to worst, I could always stow away on the helicopter. But I can cross that bridge if and when it comes. For now, there's work to be done.'

She grabbed Alex's hand. 'Thank you for suggesting this and arranging for me to join as crew. I know you went out of your way. It's exactly what I need right now.'

'As I said, anything for my best friend.'

'Okay, before we get too mushy, you should give me my orders. No desserts for lunch, but I'm sure there's still lots to do.'

A prolonged blast from the yacht alarm jolted Deepti.

'Ah, that means we're about to set sail,' Alex explained. 'If you want, you can go to the beach club sea terrace and watch as we leave England.'

'I'm good, thanks,' she replied. Then, giving a mock-salute, she said, 'Goodbye, England. See you in a few weeks.

'Come on, tell me what to do. I'd better get

a move on if we're going to have lunch ready in an hour.' She pulled up her sleeves, ready to begin her new adventure.

'Ahoy, Matteo. *Bon voyage.*'

Matteo Di Corrado shook his head at his executive assistant's effort to use sailing terms for her parting words as they signed off from their video chat. It was a shame she was staying to hold the fort in his London offices but she had told him she didn't want to sail for a month. He couldn't blame her. It wasn't his first preference either. Not at this time.

He stood up from behind his desk and turned to the large glass doors which opened onto an aft deck. He placed his palm on the access panel then, once the glass doors slid open, he stepped onto the deck. There were four areas, each with a table surrounded by six arm chairs. There were no decorative comfort features. It had been designed as an outdoor breakout area for when the yacht was used for conferences in the future, not for relaxation—unlike his private deck on the level above, which had a large hot-tub surrounded by loungers that were almost drowning in throw cushions.

With his arms folded, he watched as the coast of Southampton faded further into the distance... finally. The original plan had been to set sail that morning, but he'd taken the red-eye flight from New York and had had an early-morning meeting in London. Then another last-minute early meeting had delayed his travel down to Southampton, which meant the captain had needed to reassess his plans, and they'd departed late.

He ran a hand across the back of his neck. He needed to be at the top of his game for the complex discussions he'd be having in the afternoon's meetings. Then the guests would be arriving in the evening for business talks over dinner, and would be staying on board for further talks as they made their way to their first stop in Lisbon.

He was used to being on the go, jetting across continents at a moment's notice, but this kind of hectic schedule was one of the main reasons he'd bought *Serendipity* and converted a deck into a business suite. He needed the change of pace which, hopefully, this voyage would provide.

He breathed in the sea air and experienced a moment of calm. The cold breeze ruffled his hair, blowing his fringe into his eyes. He ran his fingers through his hair. The added benefit of working on the yacht was he wouldn't need to look and dress immaculately, the way he would in the office. His executive assistant had even commented she had only seen him in a polo shirt when he'd been on the golf course.

Naturally, he had a smart suit, shirt and tie hanging in a cupboard in his office, and a whole row in the walk-in robe which was part of his owner's suite. He would change before his afternoon meetings but otherwise he planned to stay in his casual clothes. It would be an interesting experiment, whether how he dressed affected his productivity.

*Serendipity* was making good progress towards the open waters. Although it wasn't strictly the yacht's maiden voyage, it was his first time using it as a floating place of business. He had always wanted to reduce his reliance on air travel; working on board the yacht would also give him unprecedented privacy, particularly with early stage negotiations, when he didn't want the business world to get wind of his plans.

But he hadn't expected to put those plans into action so soon. The situation with Bella and Leo had accelerated matters. His niece was the reason he was being forced to sail to Singapore in the first place. Bella categorically refused to fly, and there was no other easy way to get her from England to Singapore, where his parents were waiting for them.

His jaw tightened as he recalled his parents' refusal to fly to London so they could take the children on the yacht, which he'd put at their disposal. Instead, they'd come up with multiple excuses why it wasn't convenient for them, causing Matteo to adapt his plans to take the children to Singapore himself. He shouldn't be surprised; his parents constantly disappointed him. They had shown their true colours when they'd chosen to side with his brother over him. Matteo pressed his lips into a tight line, as he invariably did whenever he thought about what had happened.

Thankfully, his thoughts were interrupted by the intercom, signalling his temporary assistant needed to speak to him. They quickly went through the arrangements for his afternoon meetings.

'If that's all, Mr Di Corrado, I'll double-check that the video-conference room is functioning properly.'

'Thank you, Jack. And it's all right to call me "Matteo".' Matteo inwardly sighed at the look of surprise the assistant gave him. 'We're going to be working closely on this boat for weeks. There's no need for formality.'

Jack gave a brief nod of acknowledgement. 'There's a few hours until the meeting. Would you like anything to eat or drink?'

'No, thank you.' Matteo indicated his assistant could leave, then turned his attention to his computer screen. Without looking away, he added, 'Can you check that everything's in order for our guests' arrival? I've already confirmed the helicopter with the captain, but could you liaise with the head steward about everything else?'

'Of course, sir.'

Matteo could only hope Jack was a quicker study than his apparent inability to follow the instruction to call him by his first name would indicate, because he certainly didn't have time on this trip to break someone completely into his way of working.

But perhaps he was being harsh. To accommodate his executive assistant's wish to remain in England—Matteo would do anything to accommodate her, as he wasn't prepared to risk losing her—he had exchanged assistants with his company vice-president for the duration of the trip. The vice-president was from an older generation and probably insisted on honorifics. It could take Jack time to get over that habit.

Matteo turned his focus back to the spreadsheets on his screen. Within minutes, concerns about his temporary assistant and his niece and nephew were put to the back of his mind as he worked through the data.

Not thirty minutes had passed before there

was an urgent knock on the door and Jack came back into the room.

'Sir, Tracey needs to speak to you. I'm afraid there's a problem,' the assistant said.

Matteo frowned, trying to recall who Tracey was. When a lady came in carrying Leo, he realised she was the children's nanny.

'Bella's missing,' Tracey said. 'I left her playing in the play room while I put Leo down for his nap and, when I went back, she wasn't there.'

Matteo stood up immediately. 'How long ago was this?' he asked. 'Have you alerted the crew to look out for her?'

Tracey shook her head. 'It's only been five minutes, but I thought you should know immediately.

'Well, she can't have got far,' Matteo said. 'Jack, please alert the captain so he can implement any search protocols. Tracey, you should return to the play room and stay with Leo while we search.'

'You're going to search for her?' Jack asked, his voice rising in surprise.

Matteo didn't bother with a reply. Of course he was going to look for his niece. He had arranged for the whole yacht to be child-proofed as soon as he'd found out he would have to take Bella by sea. There was no access to the yacht exterior or dangerous engine rooms without additional security—either his handprint or a code—so there was no way Bella could have made it out on deck.

But, if Bella had managed to slip past her nanny, there was no telling where she could be on an eighty-metre boat. How could Tracey have left Bella on her own in new surroundings? Hadn't his parents done the proper checks when they'd hired this nanny? How difficult could it be to look after two children when one of them was practically a baby?

He had no idea what involvement his parents had had with employing a nanny for the children; he hadn't spoken to them for over six years. All communication about bringing the children to Singapore had been through intermediaries. Six years later, he still couldn't wrap his head around the fact that, despite acknowledging what his brother had done was wrong, his parents had chosen not only to keep in contact with but actively support him rather than take Matteo's side. He'd been betrayed by his whole family.

He could admit, he had no interest in talking to his parents when he handed over the children; he didn't want to see them at all. But at least that was still weeks away. Right now, he needed to concentrate on finding Bella.

Matteo spent twenty minutes searching the

lower main deck. The VIP guests' suites were large but there weren't many places a child could hide. The port-side rooms had been converted to the family rooms with the children's and nanny's bedrooms, a play room and a large entertainment suite. The crew was searching their quarters and the yacht's exterior, unsuccessfully so far. Bella wasn't anywhere.

His face was steel as he strode to the main deck. With work piling up and an imminent meeting, the last thing he needed to do was look for a missing child. If Bella was playing a game of hide and seek, she was doing very well. Since she barely spoke, he wasn't expecting her to answer him, but he called out her name anyway.

# CHAPTER TWO

AFTER LUNCH AND clean-up were over, Deepti was working in the small galley off the main dining room, putting the finishing touches to a variety of *petits fours* she'd made for dessert for the evening. She wanted to get an idea of what was popular with the guests and crew. As she was about to put the final touch of an intricate decoration on one of them, she heard movement behind her but she didn't look up, assuming it was one of the crew checking on preparations for that evening—they'd been coming in and out all afternoon.

Unusually, she sensed the visitor silently stand opposite her.

'What are you doing?' a young child's voice asked.

Not expecting that sound, Deepti squeezed her piping bag a little too tightly and too much frosting escaped, drenching the dessert. Turning the pastry in her hands, she chewed the inside of her cheek. She couldn't see an obvious way to salvage the mess. She grimaced. It wouldn't be wasted—she was sure some crew member would be happy to eat it—but she couldn't afford to make mistakes, particularly not on her first day. Hopefully, no unexpected guests would be helicoptered in that day, so there would still be plenty of her *petits fours* to go round.

While she put down her piping bag and wiped her hands on a towel at her waist, Deepti observed her visitor. Large, round brown eyes stared back at her. Deepti had no idea how old the child was, but the little girl was adorable, with those eyes and her curly brown hair. But her face was so sad. Deepti resisted an urge to give her a comforting cuddle.

She'd had very few dealings with children in her twenty-eight years. As an only child, Deepti had had no nieces or nephews to spend time with, and none of her friends were yet at that 'having children' phase. From her limited knowledge, Deepti didn't think a young child should be wandering freely round a large yacht. Where were her parents?

'Hey, have you got lost? Are you looking for your mummy and daddy?' she asked in her normal voice. Then she paused a moment. Didn't people usually speak to children in a high-pitched tone or was that just for babies? She had no idea how to engage with kids.

'No. What are you doing?' The girl repeated her earlier question.

'I'm decorating the desserts for dinner this evening.'

'Why?'

'Because they look pretty this way, don't you think?' Deepti picked up one of her perfectly decorated *petits fours* and turned it round for the girl to see.

'It's nice. Can I help you?'

Deepti looked at the remaining *petits fours*. She could spare one. She'd made enough individual pastries for each guest to have four, but hopefully at least a couple of guests wouldn't eat all their share, and she was sure the owner wouldn't count how many she'd put out to notice some were missing. And this way there would be an even number of desserts: it was one of her quirks that she preferred numbers to be even when they could be.

Perhaps if she could get the child to concentrate on the decoration she could ask her some questions and find out who she belonged to. And perhaps, if Deepti was really lucky, the girl's parents would be happy to have a badly decorated piece if their daughter had created it.

'All right, then. Let me put this tray away,' she

said, and suited her actions to her words. 'Why don't you sit over here, sweetie? What's your name?'

'Bella.'

'Okay, Bella. I'm Deepti.'

'Dippy.'

Deepti sighed. It wasn't the first time her name had been pronounced that way. At least Bella wasn't doing it deliberately to tease her.

'Deep-ti,' she enunciated. 'But you can call me Dee.'

She placed a towel around Bella's clothes to work as an apron. Then, on a plate, she showed the girl how to squeeze out the frosting. While Bella was decorating, Deepti asked her where her parents were.

'In the sky.'

'They're on a plane?' Deepti asked, surprised the girl was on the yacht when her parents were flying.

She was caught off-guard when Bella's face crumpled and tears started to fall. She took a step forward and then paused. Was it right for her to go to the girl? She wished she had more experience to know the appropriate thing to do in these circumstances. Then Deepti shook her head. Forget appropriateness. She couldn't watch a little girl cry in front of her and not offer her comfort.

'Oh, sweetie. Don't cry,' she said, stroking the girl's back. She looked around the galley and found a kitchen roll. She broke off a sheet and used it to wipe the tears. 'It's going to be okay, sweetie.' Or perhaps she shouldn't have said that. You weren't supposed to say things you didn't know you could deliver, were you? Or did that only apply to doctors and the police? Deepti had never felt so out of her depth as she did at that moment.

She closed her eyes. All this second-guessing wasn't simply because she hadn't dealt with children before. Ever since she'd worked out her ex-boyfriend must have been involved in her losing the deal and her client, she'd known she'd put her trust and belief in the wrong person. When she couldn't trust her instincts, when she couldn't trust her judgement, how could she trust herself? The unfortunate legacy of their relationship.

She grabbed the damaged *petit four*. 'Here, Bella. What do you think of this? It's a bit of a mess. Do you think you can fix it? Look.' Deepti started scraping the frosting off the pastry with her finger. Bella stopped crying as she watched her, carefully reaching out to touch the frosting.

Deepti also had the ingredients ready to make dinner rolls with her. Bella couldn't do too much damage if she helped with preparing the dough, and while she was occupied Deepti could try to find more information.

'Who's looking after you on this boat?' Deepti asked while they were sifting the flour.

'Uncle Mayo.' Bella scrunched her face up. 'And Tracey.'

Deepti couldn't remember being introduced to a Mayo or Tracey but perhaps they were part of the engineering team rather than the stewards. She needed to find Alex and ask him to contact this Mayo.

She moved towards the door, then halted. She probably shouldn't leave Bella alone in case she hurt herself or even wandered off again. But, if she didn't let someone know Bella was with her, there could be two worried guardians on the yacht.

She'd heard a lot of activity in the crew quarters and outside the boat when she'd brought the dessert from the main kitchen to this side galley. Perhaps they were searching for this little girl.

Should she take Bella out and look for someone from the crew? Deepti looked at her as she played with the mixture. It seemed a shame to interrupt her when she looked as if she was enjoying herself. Surely a member of the crew would come round soon?

A few minutes later, she thought she heard

movement in the next room, but no one came through to the galley. Thinking it could be a deck-crew member who wasn't aware there was a room behind the large mirror, Deepti moved to the dining area doorway to ensure she kept her eye on Bella.

'In here,' she called out before moving back to help Bella with her mixing.

She turned to greet the visitor. Suddenly the very small galley felt even smaller. Deepti swallowed, craning her neck to look at the man.

He was tall.

Most people were tall compared to her, at five foot three, but even so he was tall—at a guess, a few inches over six foot. Thank goodness the ceilings in the yacht were incredibly high. Although he was wearing a polo shirt, it wasn't the standard one that was the crew's uniform, nor the shirts that designated the people working on the bridge.

She definitely hadn't been introduced to this man earlier in the day. There was no way she would have forgotten him. He was probably the most stunning man she'd ever seen in the flesh. She couldn't stop staring at the perfection of his features: a strong jaw; straight, almost arrogant nose; dark-brown eyes that could have been staring deep into her soul.

She licked her lips, her mouth suddenly dry.

He exuded power and control. This was obviously a man who was used to being in charge. And equally obviously, with his unblinking stare, someone who was not happy.

'Bella, everyone has been looking for you,' he said. 'What are you doing in here? You're supposed to be in your room.'

The man hadn't raised his voice but Deepti automatically stood in front of Bella, as if she could protect her from his displeasure.

'Bella, honey, do you know who this is?' Deepti asked the girl.

'Are you suggesting I…?'

Deepti barely spared him a glance before turning back to Bella. 'Sweetie, do you know this man?'

The girl nodded. 'Uncle Mayo.' Although Bella didn't appear scared of Mayo, she wasn't rushing to greet him either.

When Deepti went to speak to Mayo, he had his back to her. 'I've found her,' he said, speaking into his phone. 'Let the steward know so he can inform the others. No, no. That's okay. She should stay with Leo. I'll bring Bella down to her.'

'It sounds like people have been looking for you,' Deepti said, stroking Bella's hair. 'Are you ready to go back with Uncle Mayo?'

Bella shook her head vehemently. 'I want to

stay here.' She glared at the man, who had finished his call and seemed to be glaring back. Deepti expelled a breath as she looked from Bella to her uncle. There was an unusual family dynamic between them but it was none of her business.

'I want to help Dippy,' Bella insisted.

'Dippy?' The man quirked an eyebrow.

'Deepti.' Suddenly something clicked. 'And your name probably isn't Mayo…'

'No, Matteo.' There wasn't even the hint of a smile at his niece's amusing mispronunciations.

Matteo? She hadn't heard that name mentioned as part of the crew. The only Matteo she'd heard of was the yacht's owner, Matteo Di Corrado. She looked over at the powerful, controlled man standing across from her. Of course it would be him. That was exactly how Deepti's luck had been going for the last few weeks.

'Hi, I'm Deepti. I'm the assistant chef, sir.' She went to stand beside Bella and put her hands on her shoulders. 'I hope you don't mind, we thought it would be fun if we did some baking together.'

'People have been looking for Bella. Didn't you notice the crew calling for her?'

Deepti gulped. She could say anything to justify herself. She hadn't known what the best thing to do was. He was rightfully angry his niece had been missing but she wanted to point out Bella had been safe. She could only hope her error of judgement didn't cost her this job. The last thing she needed was to be fired from two jobs within weeks of each other.

She gently pressed Bella's shoulders. 'Perhaps it's time for you to go with your uncle back to your room.'

'But I want to carry on helping you,' Bella said.

'Is it possible, Mr Di Corrado—sir…' Deepti began.

'Matteo,' he bit out.

Deepti cleared her throat to speak again. 'I could take her back to her room once we've put these rolls into the oven.'

He frowned. Deepti didn't need to be a genius to read Matteo's expression. He was not pleased. From everything she'd heard about the owner of the boat and the company he owned, he was an extremely successful businessman. And an extremely busy one. He probably hadn't wanted to spend time chasing after his niece.

She bit the inside of her lip. 'Bella, sweetie, I think you need to go back with your uncle now. I'm sure we can do some more baking another day.' Deepti reached over to remove the tray from Bella but was completely unprepared for small arms to grab her around the waist and hold on tightly.

'No, stay with Dippy,' Bella whined.

Deepti noticed Matteo's eyes narrow. Why was he suspicious of her? She hadn't done anything to encourage Bella's actions.

'Sorry, sweetie, I do need to go back to work.'

'Yes, Bella. Come along. Tracey's waiting for you.'

Deepti lifted her eyebrows at his tone. If she didn't know exactly how to speak to children, she at least knew barking orders at them wouldn't help the situation.

Much as Deepti didn't have a problem with having Bella stay with her for a while longer, she wasn't going to argue with the yacht's owner on her first day. Her soul would be crushed beyond repair if she got fired from another job.

'Why don't I come with you to find Tracey?' she offered to Bella. 'Then maybe I can speak to your aunt about you coming to be my helper another day?'

Bella's mouth trembled but, instead of throwing a tantrum, she gave a tight nod. Deepti breathed a sigh of relief.

'Tracey's her nanny, not her aunt,' Matteo said, looking at his watch. 'I have a video conference that should have started five minutes ago. Can you take her downstairs on your own?'

At Deepti's nod, he gave her the code for the entrance to the lower state rooms, which would now remain closed to prevent any further escapes. Without saying anything else, not even a 'see you later' to his niece, Matteo left the galley.

Deepti breathed deeply a few times, as if trying to regain the oxygen Matteo's presence had seemed to suck out of the room.

She turned back to Bella with a bright smile. 'Are you ready to go downstairs?'

Bella nodded and stood up, then giggled. 'You look funny with all the flour all over your face.'

Deepti laughed without humour. Of course she would have flour on her face when she met an incredibly gorgeous male for the first time. At least she wouldn't have to worry about being attracted to him. Even if he weren't her boss, she wasn't interested in romance or relationships. What was the point when she had incredibly bad judgement when it came to men? She would never be able to trust how she felt any more. She would rather be alone than end up getting hurt over and over again.

# CHAPTER THREE

BY SEVEN O'CLOCK the following morning, Matteo had already finished a session in the gym, followed by a quick swim, and had completed an hour of work. He stood up from his desk, ready for his first cup of coffee. His brows drew together when he realised there were no coffee-making facilities in his office suite. Since Jack wasn't around to ask, Matteo walked round the deck, checking whether a machine was hidden in some corner, without success.

Although there was a kettle in his suite, instant coffee was unappealing. He supposed it was natural some adjustments would have to be made since he was working on a yacht—he couldn't expect everything to be as organised as his usual routine demanded. But, as far as he was concerned, having the means to make his coffee was non-negotiable. He didn't have the time or patience constantly to contact Chef or a steward whenever he wanted a cup.

Although, he wouldn't object if Chef delegated that task to his assistant. Matteo paused as the image of Deepti from yesterday came to mind, her standing in front of his niece in full protective mode, her fierce stance slightly diminished by the flour on her cheeks and across her forehead. He'd had to physically restrain himself when his hand had instinctively reached out to rub his thumb across her face.

Strangely the flour had only highlighted how stunning she was. For a moment, he'd even forgotten why he'd entered the galley. He'd stood there unblinking until the sight of Bella happily playing with the dough had caught his attention.

For obvious reasons, he hadn't had much to do with Bella or Leo since they'd been born, and had limited his contact once he'd found out he would be responsible for getting them to Singapore. But he'd been told by Bella's care-givers she had withdrawn into herself after her parents had died. He'd been advised it wasn't unusual, in the circumstances, but it was something that he, or rather his parents, would need to keep an eye on.

So to have seen Bella happily working with Deepti and talking to her, when she'd barely said two words to anyone else, including her nanny, had roused his suspicions. He wasn't sure what he was suspicious about, exactly, but it wasn't

beyond the realms of possibility Deepti had specifically targeted the girl as a way to ingratiate
herself with him. He wasn't a particularly vain
man, but he knew his wealth and his looks drew
women to him, and it wouldn't be the first time
it had happened.

But he was getting ahead of himself. He
would wait to see whether there was anything
to his suspicions. If there was, Deepti would
find out soon enough he wasn't interested in
a dalliance with anyone, and definitely not a
member of his crew. And, if she was hoping
for more, for a relationship of some kind, she'd
picked the wrong candidate.

He decided to go downstairs to the dining
area where breakfast would soon be laid out
for the guests, hoping the coffee was ready
and available. At the entrance to the main state
room, he could already see there was nothing
visible on the buffet table, but Matteo could hear
some movement in the galley. Was it Deepti?
He hurried in that direction but came to a halt
when a different crew member walked out of
the galley.

'Oh, Mr Di Corrado, I wasn't expecting to see
anyone. Can I help you with something?'

Matteo didn't know who this steward was,
but he didn't have to be a genius to tell there
was a flirtatious undertone to her simple words.

He pressed his lips together. 'I'm looking for freshly brewed coffee.'

'Oh. I'm sorry, I don't know where that is. I'm only here to set up the tables, and Chef hasn't sent up anything for breakfast yet. It's going to be at least twenty minutes until we start bringing things up. I'm sure if you call down to the galley someone will bring you a cup. Or I can go downstairs and ask Chef.

'That's fine, thank you. I'll go down and ask Chef myself. Carry on.' He gave a brief nod and then turned to go back into the foyer.

'Mr Di Corrado, there's a service lift in the adjacent galley which will take you directly to the main galley below. It's probably the fastest, most direct way to get there.'

Matteo nodded in acknowledgement then went over to the lift she'd indicated. She looked as though she was getting ready to join him in the small lift, but his intentionally fierce expression must have caused her to change her mind. Was this something he needed to bring up with the captain, or was he just in a bad mood because he hadn't had his first cup of coffee yet?

Thankfully, he could smell the fresh brew as soon as he entered the main galley. The chef was giving instructions to a man as he went through the dining plans. There was no sign of Deepti, not that Matteo was particularly looking for her. He cleared his throat to announce his presence.

'Mr Di Corrado. Did you want to approve the dining menu?' Chef asked.

'No, I'm looking for coffee.' Matteo had already started to regret his impulse to go searching for a coffee himself. He should have stayed in his office and called down to the chief steward. But he liked order, and he liked his routines, and part of his routine was a cup of fresh coffee in the morning.

A buzzer sounded and, seconds later, Deepti came into the galley.

'That's the rolls ready,' she called out, coming to an abrupt halt when she noticed Matteo.

'We'll deal with these, Dee. You stay with Bella,' Chef said to her, putting a mug of coffee in front of Matteo.

Dee? There was an obvious close relationship between Chef and Deepti. But that was none of his business—he didn't have a fraternisation policy for the crew. Then he recalled exactly what Chef had said.

'Bella?' Matteo looked sharply at Deepti, who had sudden colour in her cheeks.

Why was Bella with Deepti again? Did Deepti have some scheme that involved his niece?

'Oh, please don't worry,' Deepti said. 'Bella didn't run away. Tracey brought her to me. Apparently, Bella asked to see me when she woke up.' She put a reassuring hand on his arm.

The jolt from the unexpected contact was greater than the hit from his first sip of coffee. He moved his arm so quickly, Deepti flinched.

'Where is Bella right now?' he asked.

'Um...' Deepti swallowed. Was that a sign of nerves or guilt?

'She's sitting in the crew lounge,' she continued. 'She's not alone; there are crew with her. I only left her for a moment because I knew the timer was about to go off. And I finished my meal prep before she joined me, so there won't be any delay to the guests' breakfast.' She spoke in a rush, casting nervous glances at the head chef.

Matteo shook his head. He wasn't accusing Deepti of abandoning his niece: in fact, it was the opposite. Deepti had been recruited to his yacht to carry out a job, and that job wasn't being a babysitter for Bella for the whole day.

'Make sure Bella goes back to Tracey soon. I presume you have other work to keep you occupied.' His tone was harsher than he'd intended.

Deepti flushed then looked at the ground. 'Yes, Mr Di Corrado.'

Matteo grimaced. She'd taken his tone as a chastisement when he'd been trying to make sure his niece wasn't disturbing her.

Why was Bella so drawn to the woman? Were they actually strangers? Something didn't add up. Experience had taught him people weren't to be trusted without question. Was Bella's attachment to Deepti wholly coincidental, or was he correct in suspecting it was part of some scheme? And, if it was a scheme, what kind could it be? How would befriending his niece give Deepti an advantage—unless, as had happened in the past, it was a reason to get close to him?

'Is there anything else, sir?' Chef asked. 'We have a note you'll be taking breakfast in your office. Is that still your instruction?'

'Yes.' He drank down the rest of the coffee and placed the mug near the dishwasher. He glanced at his watch. He was already half an hour behind on his day, all because he decided to get his own coffee. 'Please also ask the head steward to arrange for coffee-making facilities to be placed in the outer office.

'Of course, sir,' Chef replied.

'Deepti, take me to Bella. She needs to go back to her nanny now. Don't indulge her,' Matteo said.

Deepti's eyes widened. She looked behind her in what he assumed was the direction of the crew quarters. 'I can take Bella straight back. I'm sure you're busy, Mr Di Corrado.'

'Matteo,' he bit out. Why was she wasting his time arguing? If getting close to him had been her plan, she wasn't doing a good job of capitalising on her friendship with Bella.

'It's breakfast time in the crew lounge,' Deepti said hesitantly. She was trying to communicate some message with the look she gave him. He narrowed his eyes. He didn't have time to mess around. If she had something to say, she should just say it.

With an angry sigh, he opened his mouth to repeat his request.

'It's breakfast time,' she repeated before he could speak. 'The crew are eating now.' She flashed a quick, nervous smile, as if she was worried she'd said something out of order and feared reprisal. He closed his eyes briefly when her meaning became clear. His presence in the crew mess could be awkward. As the owner, he could technically go anywhere he wanted on board this yacht. Deepti had tried to be careful with her warning that he would be going into a space where the crew should be free to relax, and definitely eat breakfast, without him disturbing them.

He took a few seconds to observe Deepti as she finished with whatever she had been making in the oven. She was an interesting contradiction—in some ways unassuming, but not afraid to stand up to him when it came to Bella, and also not afraid to hint at how something he was planning to do might not be appropriate. She wasn't fawning on him, that was for sure. He could probably disregard the notion she had a scheme to get close to him.

He couldn't quite define the emotion he experienced at the moment—it was most likely relief.

'Very well,' he said. 'Take Bella back to her room. Then ask Tracey to make an appointment with my assistant. I want to speak to her.'

'Of course, Mr Di Corrado.'

'Matteo,' he said again as he was leaving the galley.

Bella was starting to be a problem. She couldn't expect Deepti to be at her beck and call. And Tracey needed to be able to look after both her charges without assistance. Or maybe that was the issue. Perhaps he should employ a second nanny specifically to look after Bella.

By the time he got back to his office suite, his assistant was at his desk, waiting to go through the agenda. The first meeting with his guests would be in an hour. He had a lot to get through before then…and he was ready for his second cup of coffee for the day.

# CHAPTER FOUR

LATER THAT EVENING, while the guests were at dinner, Deepti completed all the prep work she could do for the following day's meals. She'd promised Bella she would pop in to spend a little time with her before she went to bed, and if she was going to keep her promise she needed to finish up in the galley quickly.

After this evening, she probably needed to start keeping her distance from Bella. She wasn't on board to be her babysitter, as Matteo had made abundantly clear. She grimaced as she recalled how she'd annoyed him that morning. She couldn't afford to do anything to jeopardise this job.

It had been a completely lucky break when Alex had called her with the offer— a month away from her troubles to regroup and decide what to do next. How to clear her name was the priority. But that wouldn't be possible if she was sent off the yacht at the first port they docked at because she wasn't spending her time on her work, or because she simply irritated the yacht's owner.

Sometimes, when Deepti saw the lounges and bedrooms, she forgot she was on a boat. They were bigger than the rooms in her parents' house. Her entire London flat could probably fit in the main salon. The playroom and children's bedrooms were cheerful, with their vibrant, primary colours. Deepti had assumed Matteo wouldn't care much about the children's area, but the amount of toys and play things available showed he'd spared no expense in making sure the children would be comfortable during the voyage.

Deepti spent an hour playing with Bella before the little girl fell asleep on her lap as they were reading together on one of the bean bags in the playroom. Deepti lay there for a while, unsure whether to take Bella to her room or wait for Traccy to return. From the awkward position she was in, she probably wouldn't be able to get up without waking Bella, so she remained seated, holding the little girl closer.

She heard a noise in the foyer and looked up to see Matteo enter the state room. The previous times she'd seen him, he'd been dressed casually in a polo shirt and chinos, and he'd been a walking Adonis in those simple clothes. But in a form-fitting, superbly tailored jacket, he looked as if he had walked straight off a catwalk. It was all she could do to stop herself whistling in reverent appreciation.

Suddenly, she became aware of him calling her name. 'What? Sorry.' She tore her gaze from his broad chest and looked down at Bella instead to gather her thoughts.

She became acutely aware of how awkward she must look, splayed out on the bean bag. First, flour on her face, now this. She should probably reconcile herself to never looking her best in his presence.

'I asked where Tracey is,' Matteo said.

'In the bathroom. I told her to take a wash after she put Leo down for the night. When she gets back, I'll help her put Bella down and then go back to my duties.' Not that she had anything left to do that night, but she didn't want to give him the slightest reason to think she was shirking her work. 'Tracey shouldn't be too long. Shall I ask her to find you when she's out?' It was really difficult to maintain a dignified attitude when she was splayed on a bean bag with a child covering her.

He waved his hand. 'There's no need. I spoke to her earlier. How long have you been with Bella?'

'About an hour. After I finished prepping for tomorrow.'

He narrowed his eyes.

Deepti worried her bottom lip. Had she said something wrong?

'Normally, what you do with your free time is up to you. However, I would like to speak to you this evening—about Bella. When do you think you'll be free?'

'Tracey shouldn't be too long. I'm sure I'll be able to leave here within half an hour.'

'Good. I'll speak to you then.'

He was almost at the door before Deepti remembered to ask where he would be. Her shoulders sagged in relief when he told her to go to the upper-deck lounge. She didn't really want to be seen by any of the guests—there was a strong possibility some of them could be from the financial sector. She couldn't take the risk of bumping into anyone who might know her, or even of her.

If Matteo found out she'd been fired from her previous job, and under a cloud of suspicion for unethical behaviour, he might be unhappy to have her employed on *Serendipity* when there were business guests coming and going.

He nodded and left. Almost immediately, her thoughts started whirring with concern about what he wanted to speak to her about. The only thing she knew was it couldn't be anything good.

Twenty minutes later, she was making her way to the upper deck, taking the crew stairs to avoid all the guests. Once she reached the floor, she listened carefully for any sounds before going into the foyer, in case Matteo was with someone.

She knocked on the door of the outer office, but there was no response. She cautiously opened the door and walked inside. Both the outer office and the main office were dimly lit and quiet. There was no sign of Matteo or his assistant Jack.

She glanced at her watch. She had told Matteo it could be half an hour before she was able to come up so, since she was early, he could still be socialising with his guests.

She went back out into the foyer. Across from the offices was the main business suite she'd seen on her first day. The door to that side was closed and there didn't seem to be any lights on to indicate someone was waiting there.

She stood in the foyer for a few minutes and then remembered he'd asked to meet her in the upper-deck lounge, which was a room off Matteo's office. She went back through the offices to a salon which had a large L-shaped sofa across from a wall-mounted television. It was probably the most snug room on the boat with, unexpectedly, a lot of space taken up by a staircase which she assumed gave direct access to the owner's deck.

Although the lights were on in the lounge, it was empty. She called out in case there was a hidden room but, when no response came, she turned to go back to the foyer and was almost through Matteo's office when she heard a voice.

'Deepti. There you are.' She whirled round at the deep voice behind her, almost tripping over her feet in her surprise.

'I didn't mean to startle you,' Matteo said, putting a hand on her arm to help steady her.

Every nerve in her skin flared into high alert. 'I'm fine,' she said, moving away. He must have come down the stairs without her hearing, but she knew his sudden appearance wasn't the reason for her heightened response to his touch.

'I wasn't expecting you to be down here,' he said, leading her to the staircase and putting his hand out to request she should go up ahead of him.

'Isn't this the upper-deck lounge?' she asked, puzzled, indicating the room they were in.

He didn't answer and she didn't press. She would need to check what the decks were called with Alex or another member of the crew, so she didn't look so incompetent in the future.

'Take a seat,' Matteo said, gesturing to the sofas and arm chairs surrounding a dark-wood coffee table.

Deepti had never thought of furniture as gendered before, but she would have known instantly the room was for a man. There were no scatter pillows or purely decorative pieces on the sofas, and the coffee table was bare, not even an artistically placed photobook in view. There was a decanter and Scotch glasses on a bar made of glass and aluminium. Every instinct told her the modern décor should clash with the older-style coffee table and seating, but it didn't at all. Whoever had designed and decorated the interiors on *Serendipity* was a genius.

'How about a drink?' Matteo asked, once she had chosen to take an arm chair.

Deepti took a deep breath. 'Of course, what would you like?' she asked, getting ready to stand to carry out her crew duties.

Matteo laughed, the sound making her heart do little flips. Deepti's eyes became round. Where had her reaction come from?

'I can pour the drinks,' he replied. 'You don't need to wait on me. You're off the clock now. Stay where you are. Would you prefer a soft drink? Or the wine fridge is well stocked, and there appears to be Scotch or brandy.'

'I'm good, thank you, sir.'

Matteo looked over at her. 'What is it with people not being able to call me by my name?'

'Pardon?' She wasn't sure she'd heard him correctly. Alex had pointed out the level of formality on yachts varied between owners and, since none of them had ever crewed for Matteo before, they were all learning his preferences as they went.

Her slight discomfort came from recalling how Alex had mentioned Matteo's earlier command to call him by his first name had been to her specifically. At that time, Alex had teased her that he hadn't asked anyone else to call him Matteo. Being asked to call someone by their first name wasn't something to make a big deal of. She always called her bosses by name and, although she initially maintained a level of formality with her clients, she used their first names too whenever they invited her to.

The lighting in the room was low but enough to illuminate Matteo at the bar. She couldn't take her eyes off his strong arms and elegant hands as he moved efficiently to pour his drink. The image of his arm gathering her around the waist and drawing him to her popped into her mind. She coughed to dispel the image. She needed to get her thoughts and reactions under control.

It was the room: the atmosphere was too romantic for her liking. And romance was the last thing on her mind, particularly after the way her last relationship had ended. This was a work meeting, after all. Would he think it was strange if she asked him to make the lights brighter?

Luckily, without her having to say anything, Matteo increased the light as he came to sit across from her.

'Was Bella okay when you left?' he asked.

'Yes, still sleeping peacefully. I hope you don't mind that I spent time with her. I promise she wasn't in the way, and I did get all my work done.'

Matteo pressed his lips together. Did that mean he did mind?

'You've probably heard the situation with Bella and Leo,' he said, staring at his glass as he twirled the liquid in it.

'I know they're your niece and nephew and you're taking them to Singapore. But that's all,' she answered truthfully.

'But you've no doubt noticed Bella doesn't speak much.'

Deepti shrugged. 'Not really.'

'Hmm.'

What did that sound mean?

'You haven't noticed?' he asked, sitting forward with a curious expression.

'To be honest, I don't know how much children are supposed to speak. I mean, she is quiet, but she can hold conversations and sometimes, when we're playing a game or talking about her favourite shows, she can be quite chatty.' Deepti puffed out her cheeks—she had never expected to be having the same conversations on repeat as much as she had with Bella.

'That's unusual.'

'Pardon?' Deepti asked.

'From what I've been told, Bella hasn't spoken much to anyone since her parents died. It's unusual that you say she talks to you.'

At first Deepti bristled at the implication she was lying about Bella chatting to her, then her mouth fell open as she realised the full extent of what Matteo had said.

'Her parents died? The poor mite.' She was quiet for a moment, thinking about the children who would have to grow up without their parents. Little Leo probably would have no memory of them. And now their uncle was taking them to their grandparents in a new country. No wonder the little girl had burst into tears when Deepti had asked about her parents.

'Oh, so that's what she meant by her parents being in the sky. I thought she meant they were in a plane.'

'Bella won't fly at all. Not since her parents died. I wonder whether sky and flying and heaven have become confused in her mind in some way.'

Deepti didn't respond. She was no child psychologist, so she wasn't going to offer an opinion. Her heart went out to the children, and to Matteo too. As Bella was his niece, it meant Matteo's brother or sister had passed away. She covered her mouth briefly. 'I'm so sorry for your loss.'

He waved away her condolences.

'You appear to be one of the only people Bella engages with,' Matteo said.

'I don't know why. Do I resemble one of her parents?'

Matteo's laugh was grim. 'Not even remotely. Bella looks like her mother. She was very beautiful.'

'Okay,' Deepti replied. Her lips twitched… Had Matteo meant to insult her own looks? 'What was she like before her parents died? Was she quiet then?'

'I don't know. I wasn't in touch with them.'

'With your brother?' She figured he would have mentioned if Bella's mother, who was very beautiful, had been his sister.

'That's right.'

His curt response warned Deepti not to question that further, but she couldn't deny her curiosity was aroused. There was silence for a few minutes as Matteo took a few drinks from his Scotch.

'Bella likes your company,' he said finally, putting his glass down on a coaster on the coffee table. 'She hasn't responded to Tracey the way she has to you, and it's making things difficult for Tracey to balance taking care of Bella and Leo at the same time. I would like you to consider being Bella's companion until we reach Singapore.'

'Her companion?' Deepti beamed. What a relief she wasn't in trouble for spending time with Bella, but instead was being invited to spend more time with her. 'I'm very happy to spend time with Bella when I'm not on duty.'

Matteo swallowed and blinked a couple of times. He shook his head, as if clearing some unexpected, unwelcome, thought. Then he said, 'No, I'm not asking you to take on additional duties. I know you passed the background checks I required for all crew, since you're sailing with children on board, so there's no concern there. I did consider hiring another nanny to take sole care of Bella but there would be a risk Bella wouldn't respond to a new person either. I already know she likes you. It makes sense for you to become her companion.'

Deepti expelled a breath. She wouldn't know how to take on that role. Just because Bella had spoken to her the last couple of days didn't mean she would continue in the future. It could be the baking that engaged Bella. She said as much to Matteo, adding that she didn't have any qualifications to be a nanny.

'Maybe Bella is just enjoying the baking with you, but I doubt that's all, since you've been together when you're not in the kitchen,' he replied. 'And I'm not asking you to be her nanny, but her companion. Bella needs a friend right now. You can be that friend.'

'But I can be her friend and carry on with my work as assistant chef. I'm sure Alex wouldn't mind.'

Matteo's jaw tightened, making her worry about contradicting him further. 'I would prefer you concentrate on Bella. I already spoke to Chef and he is fine with you taking this role. He has asked whether you can continue to assist with desserts and pastries, and I'm sure that will be no problem for me, but if it does turn out to be too much work for you, you can let me know. I understand you're *cordon bleu* qualified as a pastry chef, so it would be foolish not to use your talent when I'm entertaining guests. When there aren't any guests on board, I don't need desserts.'

Deepti nibbled her bottom lip. It was true she did have a qualification, but she was certain Alex hadn't informed Matteo that she had never worked as a chef or in a kitchen in any capacity before.

She'd already been terrified of messing up as an assistant chef and now she was being asked to take on a completely different role, one she had no qualifications or experience for.

She didn't have any other arguments, apart from her intense worry that she would fail at the role. She didn't know whether her self-worth could take losing another job, especially not immediately after having been fired from the previous one.

'I've also asked Chef and the head stew to add another assistant chef once we get to Lisbon, so you don't need to worry about your duties being a burden on the others.'

'It sounds like you've thought of everything. I'm guess I'm not really in a position to say no.'

His face hardened. 'No! You *are* in a position to say no. I'm not forcing you to take this role. You were hired as a galley assistant—if you want to keep your current job, that's acceptable and understandable.'

'Then what will you do about Bella and Tracey?'

If it was possible, his face got even tighter, as if he were sucking lemons. 'We will have to manage somehow. It's not something you would need to worry about. In any event, my parents will need to consider the situation once we get to Singapore. I'll send them a message.'

Deepti was struck by his unusual choice of words—sending a message rather than speaking to them directly. There was something more to the situation. But it wasn't any of her business, unless it was relevant to the issue of Bella.

'Would it help if I understand some of her background? What happened to her parents?'

Matteo didn't reply immediately. He drank more of his Scotch. She was sure he was swallowing down some indefinable emotion with the alcohol.

'I hope you understand, it's a family matter. I don't think it's necessary or appropriate to go into details unless you accept the position.'

'Understood,' Deepti replied. 'And I appreciate you haven't tried to guilt-trip me into taking on the role,' she added without thinking.

Matteo blinked in surprise at her response. Had she been too flippant?

'Bella's a five-year-old girl,' Matteo said after a minute. 'She deserves to have a companion who likes spending time with her, not someone who is acting out of guilt or financial motives. That's why I asked you and didn't simply hire someone to join the yacht.'

Colour rushed to her cheeks. She was on the

precipice of annoying Matteo and she couldn't afford to do that. She felt stuck between a rock and hard place. She was crewing as an assistant chef, a role she had no experience in, and now she was being asked to take on a different role as a child's companion—another role she was supremely unqualified for.

Whatever she decided, it could end up badly for her. She couldn't bear to make any more mistakes. But could she trust herself to make the right decision?

# CHAPTER FIVE

THE FOLLOWING DAY, Matteo stood on the deck watching the helicopter take his guests back to shore. The meetings had been successful, and being able to conduct them without any interruptions and in complete privacy had provided an added benefit. So far, conducting his business on *Serendipity* was working out well. Now he had a clear day free from meetings before they docked at Lisbon that evening.

Matteo knew his assistant was inside, waiting to go through some papers with him. If he'd begun straight away, he'd have been able to accomplish a lot before taking a break for lunch. Instead, he was on deck thinking about his conversation with Deepti the previous night.

He'd given her until the afternoon to make her decision. What would it be? He could understand her wariness at taking on a role for which she had no experience but he wasn't asking for a childcare expert, only someone to be a friend to Bella. Someone who Bella could, hopefully, open up to. From what he'd observed, Deepti was the natural choice.

And if she didn't agree? He'd told her he wouldn't force her and that was true. But he'd never said he wouldn't try to persuade her to change her mind. He'd already countered most of her objections when offering her the job, but he needed to think about additional inducements. He couldn't explain why, but he was certain that an increase in salary wouldn't be a sufficient incentive.

'Mr Di Corrado?' his assistant called, coming onto the deck. 'An email has just come through. I think you should take a look...'

Matteo nodded and made his way back inside. It was better to concentrate on work rather than think about Deepti—about what would persuade Deepti to take on the new role.

By the time he stopped for lunch, Matteo had caught up on most of the work that had been delayed from the previous day while he'd searched for Bella. Usually, when he was in his London office, his executive assistant brought him lunch to eat at his desk, but part of the reason for him to trial running his business from the yacht was to introduce more balance into his working life. He decided he'd take a proper break and eat in the main dining area. He assumed food would continue to be served there unless his assistant had told them to stop.

He would ask Deepti to join him for coffee after lunch so he could ask her about his job offer. It would be more convenient for him if he didn't have to make time during his hectic afternoon to schedule an appointment with her.

When he got to the main salon, he heard a noise from the galley. He walked over to see who was in there, when a steward came out with Bella. He felt relief it wasn't the flirtatious steward but it was a shame it wasn't Deepti. It would be convenient if he didn't have to send for her. He had no interest in Deepti beyond that—he was used to working with very attractive people.

He walked over to the buffet to see what dishes were on offer. Bella started helping the steward lay the table. She looked comfortable and happy, putting the cutlery down carefully, then straightening it.

Had he made a mistake? Was Bella happy to be with anyone and only acting out against Tracey? He had been sure there was something special between Bella and Deepti.

'Bella, where's Tracey?' he asked.

Bella gave him a quick glance then continued her task.

'Tracey went to put Leo down for his nap,' the steward replied.

'And she left Bella with you?' he asked with a frown.

'Ah, no.' The steward was interrupted by Deepti coming out from the galley, carrying a tray.

'Here it is, sweetie. A special meal just for you,' she called out before stopping short when she noticed Matteo. 'Sorry, I didn't realise you would be eating in the dining room today.' She put the tray on the buffet then went to stand next to Bella. 'Hey, poppet, why don't we go back to your special room and eat there?'

Bella shook her head. 'I want to eat here.'

Matteo noticed that, besides cutlery for him, a place had been set with a child's fork and knife.

With a nod towards him and Deepti, the steward left.

'I'm so sorry, Matteo,' Deepti said. 'I hadn't got the message that you were eating in the main dining room today. Bella said she wanted to eat her lunch like all the important guests,' Deepti said, giving him the sweetest smile as she repeated what his niece had said. 'And I assumed it would be empty. We'll leave you to eat in peace.'

Matteo looked at his niece, who was already climbing onto a chair next to him.

'It's fine, Deepti, she can eat here.'

'Are you sure?'

He bit down his impatience. Why did she

need the reassurance? He caught the tightness in her eyes. She was really anxious about disturbing him. Was he that scary? 'Honestly, Deepti. It's fine.'

Her smile of relief was like the sun coming out on a cloudy day, which was a ridiculously fanciful simile—he had no idea why he'd thought of it.

'Thank you,' Deepti said. 'Shall I have your tray sent to your office?'

That would be the wisest choice. He could work while he ate and try to catch up on lost time. Deepti placed a reassuring hand on Bella's shoulder as she waited expectantly for his reply. He presumed she would stay with Bella while she ate, which would save time again.

He sat down. 'I can eat here too.'

Bella clapped her hands. 'Yes, Uncle Mayo and I eat like the important people.'

His look of shock was reflected in Deepti's expression.

Admittedly, he hadn't spent much time with the girl before, but this was the first time she'd acknowledged him in a friendly manner.

Bella patted the seat next to her, so Deepti carried Bella's tray over. 'Would you like me to bring the dishes over?' Deepti asked him.

'That's fine, I can serve myself.' He walked over to the buffet and started piling food onto his plate. 'Shall I get you a plate while you help Bella?'

Deepti looked horrified. 'Oh no, thank you, sir.'

So it was back to 'sir'… Rather than remind her to use his first name, he asked, 'Have you had lunch? Isn't it your break?'

'Yes, but I'll eat later. Once Bella's back with Tracey.'

'There's plenty of food here.'

'But that food's been made for you and Jack.'

His jaw clenched. She was being unnecessarily obstinate about something insignificant, but it wasn't a battle that was worth his time to fight. It was clear Chef was preparing different meals for him than for the crew, but that wasn't necessary, when there were only five people who weren't crew on board and two of those were children. He would have a word with the captain and head chef when he had some free time.

'Do you want to watch *Pets in Petland* with me, Uncle Mayo?' Bella asked.

'It's a kids' programme,' Deepti explained when he turned to her. 'I watched a few episodes yesterday. It's very good.' There was laughter in her tone which suggested the opposite.

He couldn't help returning her grin before saying, 'I'm afraid I have a lot of work to do once I've finished eating.'

Bella looked crestfallen. 'Daddy was always busy too.'

He felt a stab of some undefinable emotion go through him at hearing his brother referred to as 'Daddy'. After that, Bella only spoke to Deepti. Although Deepti did keep trying to bring him into the conversation, Bella refused even to look in his direction.

'Why don't we watch some of your pets programme in the evening, just before bed time?' he found himself saying. 'If you want, we can watch it in the big cinema room.'

Bella smiled and clapped her hands again. 'Yay.'

His face broke into a grin when he caught Deepti's expression of admiration. He stopped smiling immediately—there was no reason for him to be pleased by her approval. 'Please do join us for food,' he said and then, being completely underhand, he said, 'Bella, don't you want Deepti to eat with us?'

'Yes,' Bella answered. 'Dippy is an important person like Uncle Mayo and me.'

He gave Deepti an expectant look. His lips twitched; he was sure she rolled her eyes before she walked over to fill her plate. And he was sure she was getting a small measure of revenge when she encouraged Bella to tell him, in minute detail, about some of her favourite episodes of the pet show.

They were about to start their coffee when Tracey arrived to take Bella downstairs for her nap. He signalled to Deepti to remain seated when she was about to leave too. It was a good opportunity to ask whether she had made her decision.

'I'm happy to help out as Bella's companion,' she said, slowly. 'If you're sure you are happy to hire another assistant chef, then I'll take on the job.' She paused, then she jutted out her chin in a gesture of determination. 'On one condition.'

Matteo raised his eyebrows. She had a condition for *him*?

'And that would be?' he asked.

Deepti rested her chin in her hands. 'Bella enjoyed having lunch with you. It seems to me that it could help if you spend more time with her. Well, her and Leo. I think you should play with her or read to her when you can. I know it will be difficult when you have visitors, but perhaps around her bed time. That's my condition.' She'd spoken quickly, in a rush to get her demands out without interruption.

Matteo pressed his lips together. No, he didn't think that was a good idea. Bella was a constant reminder of his brother's betrayal. She looked exactly like her mother. But that wasn't the problem, because Matteo hadn't spent much time thinking about his brother or sister-in-law in the six years of their estrangement.

The problem was he was busy. Several deals were at a critical stage and being on the yacht instead of flying, while having its advantages, also meant some things had to happen at a much slower pace.

'You've already agreed to watch *Pets in Petland* with her,' Deepti pointed out.

He still had no idea what had possessed him to do that—he had planned to go on land once they docked that evening. But there was something about Bella's crestfallen expression. Whatever had happened between his brother and him, hadn't been Bella's fault. She was an innocent child. If Deepti thought it could help, then he was willing to give it a try.

'I'll make time to spend with Bella. But you'll need to be there too.'

'Oh, I don't know if that's necessary,' Deepti began.

'Before you came into the dining room, Bella didn't engage with me at all. It would be helpful if you could be there, at least to begin with.'

Deepti stared at him intently, not saying anything. Then she nodded. 'Of course; that makes sense,' she said.

'So we have an agreement?' he asked, putting out his hand.

'We have an agreement,' she replied, clasping it.

He flexed his hand after releasing hers, still feeling that brief warmth. Making time for Bella would have the added advantage of inevitably getting to spend more time with Deepti.

But not because of her beauty, or at least not just because of that. She intrigued him and he wanted to know what it was that was catching his interest. He had discarded his earlier theory that she was using Bella to get closer to him, but that didn't mean she didn't have some other agenda. He trusted his instincts and they were telling him there was more to Deepti than met the eye. It was for that reason he wanted to get to know her better.

# CHAPTER SIX

A FEW DAYS LATER, Deepti was putting the children's lounge back in order after a day of playing with Bella. She had no idea why any room needed so many scatter cushions, but Bella liked making forts with them, so at least they served some kind of purpose.

She was probably the most exhausted she'd ever been. Who could have guessed that looking after a five-year-old was so much work? She laughed to herself—parents and care-givers everywhere would probably roll their eyes at her naivety.

Once she had finished, she sat in front of the bookcase to select a couple of books to read with Bella before she went to bed.

It had been less than a week but they had already settled into a decent routine. The only negative point was Matteo's failure to fulfil his side of the bargain. She'd been able to understand and make excuses for him while they'd been docked at Lisbon and he had been staying on land for various meetings, but since they'd set sail again she couldn't deny she was disappointed—for Bella's sake. Personally, she wasn't expecting to see him, so it didn't matter that she hadn't spoken to him since she'd agreed to take on the role of Bella's companion.

And the good thing about being constantly occupied was that she didn't have any time to think about the mess back home. One day she would need to start looking for a new job, and hopefully find a way to clear her name, but she still had a little time before she needed to worry about that. She was too bruised to deal with that at the moment.

She still couldn't understand, couldn't believe, what had happened. She'd worked in that job since she'd graduated from university—she'd done her graduate training programme there. She'd thought a promotion to director level would be her next step. Instead she'd lost a deal, which would have cost her a bonus, and immediately afterwards a high-value client had left and she'd been fired under the guise of restructuring. Colleagues with whom she'd worked closely had been ready to rush to judgement, with the inference she had acted unethically. One of her biggest mistakes had been putting her trust in the wrong person: her ex-boyfriend. It wasn't a mistake she wanted to repeat.

'Has Bella already gone to sleep?' Matteo's deep voice broke into her thoughts.

Her breath caught when Matteo's broad frame filled the doorway. She licked her lips, her throat suddenly dry.

'No.' Her reply came out as a croak. She coughed then said, 'Tracey's giving her a bath. You're right on time to read a bed-time story with her.'

He didn't acknowledge her comment but took a seat next to her on the sofa.

'Is that what you're reading with Bella this evening?' Matteo asked with a slight quirk of his lips.

Deepti looked down at the book she was reading. She'd brought it with her to read while she babysat the children later that evening but had picked it up while she'd waited for Tracey to finish. 'Absolutely! Have to start her on the classics early.'

He stifled a laugh. 'That's a classic, is it?'

She shrugged. 'Well, it's a classic of its genre.'

Matteo held out his hand. With a puzzled frown, she handed over her book, assuming he wasn't asking to hold her hand, although she'd been tempted to pretend she didn't understand his gesture.

'"A gripping psychological thriller with twists

you'll never see coming",' he said, reading the cover blurb. 'Is it any good?'

'Well, I haven't got very far yet, but I've loved all her other books, so I expect it to be excellent. I'm looking forward to getting stuck into it tonight.'

'Is that your plan for the evening? A quiet night reading?'

'That's right,' Deepti replied. 'The crew are having their weekly fun and games night on the lower deck but I'm babysitting.'

'Don't you want to join them?'

'Somebody has to stay with the children, and Tracey hasn't had the night off since we got to Lisbon.'

Before they could talk further, Bella rushed into the room and climbed onto Deepti's lap. Deepti gave her a quick cuddle then moved her onto the sofa to sit between Matteo and her. She handed him a large selection of children's books. After Bella had read three books with Matteo and Deepti, she was dropping off.

Deepti took her to tuck her up in bed. When she returned to the living area, she was surprised to see Matteo still there, leafing through her book. She'd expected him to leave as soon as Bella was asleep.

'You know there's a library on board?' he said after she sat down.

She grinned, 'I did not know that. But why should I be surprised when you have a spa with massage rooms downstairs?'

He ran a hand over his face. 'When I bought this yacht, it was with the intention of spending a considerable proportion of the year on board. I don't know... I'm always on the go. I wanted to get some peace. But, at the same time, I can't simply leave work for weeks at a time. This was a way of getting some balance—more important than ever. Life can change quickly.' He opened his eyes suddenly.

It took a while for Deepti to respond, her mind still processing Matteo's admission. Even though the companies she'd worked with were billion-pound corporations, she hadn't usually engaged with the most senior executives on a day-to-day basis, and definitely not on a social level. She couldn't imagine anyone she'd liaised with in her field giving up the hustle culture for the slow serenity of sailing on a yacht, regardless of how huge the yacht might be.

'Are there children's books in your library?' Deepti asked.

'I'm not sure. I wanted the children's things to be contained in their suite.'

'Well, Bella loves the books you have for them. She loves to read. Did she read a lot with her parents?'

'I don't know.'

'I guess liking books is something we have in common, as well as baking.'

'It is interesting that she opens up to you,' Matteo remarked.

'I'm glad she does. But I don't know why. Maybe it's because we're almost the same size,' Deepti replied with a grin. 'She may think I'm a little kid.'

'You're nothing like a kid,' Matteo declared.

Something flared in his eyes, as he stared directly into hers, that made her think he wasn't talking about her height. She blinked to break their connection.

'For all I know,' Matteo continued, 'She could always have been quiet. The main thing is she seems to be happy spending time with you. And what about you? Are things working out for you?'

'Yes, so far so good.'

Again, there was the smallest hint that there was a story behind his brother and him. She didn't know Matteo that well, barely at all, but she couldn't imagine him being the kind of person to have no relationship with his nephew and niece without a good reason. But maybe she was giving him more credit than he deserved. The reality was, she didn't know him that well at all; they'd only met a few days ago.

They were quiet for a moment. Matteo's lips

quirked. 'Thanks for not scolding me for not keeping to my part of the agreement.'

'You're a busy man. And you were here today, so it doesn't strike me that you're deliberately shirking.'

'I'm going to adjust my schedule to include time with Bella. It's just going to take a little time.'

She gave a nod of approval. 'I understand. It sounds like you have a lot on and, from what I can gather, you weren't expecting to have to take Bella by sea.'

Matteo stretched his neck. 'The way this conversation is heading, it looks like it needs some wine. I'm guessing there isn't any in the children's suite. I think I'll go up to get a bottle,' he said, standing up. His polo shirt lifted up slightly, exposing a taut stomach and abs. Deepti couldn't tear her eyes away until he asked, 'Do you prefer white or red?'

'Oh, none for me, thanks. I'm not sure it's a good idea for me to drink when I'm babysitting.' It was probably also not a good idea to have alcohol when she was already having a strong physical reaction to him. 'You don't have to keep me company. I'm sure you have more important things to do.'

Matteo looked at her with an inscrutable expression.

'Okay,' he said, then left the room.

Okay? What did okay mean? He hadn't wished her goodnight. Did that mean he was planning to come back or had he momentarily lost the courteous manner she'd observed up to that point?

She couldn't decide whether she wanted him to return or not. They hadn't spent much time together before, but she'd enjoyed chatting with him this evening and watching him while he interacted with Bella. And she couldn't deny he was very easy on the eye.

As long as that was all it was—an objective acknowledgement that Matteo was an attractive male. She wasn't interested in him for a relationship. She wasn't interested in relationships at all—not after what had happened with her ex-boyfriend.

It wasn't that she was heartbroken after her boyfriend had broken things off, but they'd been together for almost a year. She'd trusted him and it was now clear her trust had been misplaced. She couldn't imagine being so foolishly trusting again. If she could spend that much time with someone and not pick up on what he was really like, what did that tell her about her ability to trust her own judgement? She wouldn't risk putting her trust in the wrong people again, so romance and relationships were out of the question.

Not that either was in question with Matteo. He was her boss. Well, not technically: he'd told her when she'd taken the job as Bella's companion she was in his parents' employment, the same as Tracey. But that was besides the point.

Matteo was an attractive man. She could see that objectively, and it would remain objectively. Why was she even thinking of Matteo and romance at the same time? There was no indication he was interested in her or wanted to spend time with her outside their time with Bella. And she didn't want a relationship either so why were her thoughts even going in that direction?

The only reason she was in Matteo's company was because she was Bella's companion and that should be the only thing of importance. If things didn't work out, it wouldn't be fair to expect Alex to fire the new assistant chef simply for Deepti to get her old job back, so things had to work out.

Deepti stretched her legs out on the sofa, settled back against the arm and opened her book.

Less than ten minutes later, Matteo came back into the room.

'Am I interrupting?' he asked.

'I thought you'd left to get a drink.'

He held up a bottle. 'I brought it with me.

But, if I'm disturbing you, I can go back to my rooms.'

'No, of course not.' She was about to put her legs onto the floor when Matteo held up a hand, suggesting she didn't need to. He took an arm chair opposite her.

'My assistant has joined the crew's games night. Are you sure you don't want to go? I can stay here. I'll even forgo the wine.'

'Oh, thank you,' she replied. It was an incredibly generous suggestion, since it would restrict what he would be able to do. 'I'm fine staying here. Why don't you join them?'

He gave an embarrassed shrug. 'This is the crew's free time. I don't want them to feel uncomfortable or on edge because the owner's there.'

Her mouth dropped open at his explanation—she hadn't expected him to think about the comfort of the others. There was no reason for her to be that surprised—he'd shown how thoughtful he was when he'd asked her to be Bella's companion and hired an assistant chef so Alex wouldn't be under-staffed.

She wanted to get to know this gorgeous, considerate man better. To cover that alarming thought, she cleared her throat and said, 'That's probably a good idea. The crew could feel like they'd have to let you win all the games.'

'Believe me, nobody would have to *let* me win.'

She answered his wide grin with one of her own. They stared at each other for a few seconds before Deepti forced her gaze to the floor. She was tempted to tell him she'd changed her mind—not because she wanted to join the games but, with seeing Matteo as an attractive male, she wasn't sure whether being alone with him was the most sensible thing.

She sat up, suddenly feeling awkward, having her legs stretched out in front of him. He was her sort-of boss; it wasn't proper for her to sit in such an informal position. As long as she remembered he only saw her as a sort-of employee, everything should be okay.

'Why don't you have a soft drink to keep me company?' Matteo asked. 'There should be a drinks fridge somewhere in this room.'

Deepti grinned. 'There is.' She indicated the cupboards behind the dining table. 'It's hidden in one of those, but the drinks are more suitable for children.'

'How about some juice, then? Or I'll get you something from the upstairs bar.'

'I'll get some juice,' she said, starting to rise.

'You stay where you are. I can get it. Despite what you and the crew seem to think, I'm quite capable of getting things for myself.'

'I very much doubt anyone thinks you're incapable of anything. But we all have our roles to do.'

Matteo didn't respond as he poured a drink then handed it to her.

'That's an interesting point you make,' he said as he sat down.

'Is it?' She was just stating a fact.

Rather than continue on that topic, Matteo started talking about the planned stops for the rest of the journey, which led to a chat about places they had visited and a wish list of countries to travel to. The conversation flowed easily without any awkward moments.

Perhaps an hour later, Matteo pulled his phone out of his trouser pocket. Deepti couldn't help warming at his thoughtfulness at turning off the sound and putting it on vibrate so the ringing didn't wake the children.

'Please excuse me,' he said, taking a glance at the number. 'This is our California office. I'd better take this call.' He answered and immediately asked the caller to hold before turning back to Deepti. 'This will probably take a while, so I'll wish you goodnight.'

'Night.' Deepti forced out a breath after he walked out of the room. Spending time with Matteo had been an unexpected treat. He was nothing like the ruthless businessman she'd imagined when she'd first looked into him. It wouldn't be a hardship to spend more time with him, particularly since this evening had shown that she should keep her attraction under control.

The next day, Matteo made his way to the lower deck after he'd finished his afternoon meeting. He had promised to spend time with Bella, as a condition of Deepti agreeing to be Bella's companion, and he wouldn't be keeping his end of the deal if he only saw Bella for a few minutes in the evening when she was tired and ready for bed. He'd asked Jack to rearrange meetings so he had an hour each afternoon to spend with Bella while they were on board.

And it would be good to observe Bella and Deepti together closely. He wanted Bella to open up to someone but he needed to be careful she didn't form too close an attachment to Deepti. Their time together would end as soon as they reached Singapore.

He could hear laughter coming from the wraparound deck that surrounded the children's suite, so he made his way there. Bella was in the kids' pool with Traccy while Deepti was sitting on a lounger to the side. He went over to her. She must have heard him approach because she lifted her finger to her lips and indicated a sleeping Leo in her arms.

Leo's head was resting on Deepti's chest, making Matteo acutely aware of her curves displayed by her bikini top.

He hastily looked over at the pool. 'Why isn't he in his bed?' he whispered.

'We haven't had a chance to go back in yet. Bella loves being in the water but she refused to go in unless I stayed here with her.'

'You aren't swimming?'

'I was, but when Leo got tired it made more sense for Tracey to stay in the water with Bella because she's got safety training.'

When he glanced at Deepti again, he had a strong urge to hand her a towel or dressing gown. She was far to enticing for his peace of mind.

Instead, he sat on a lounger and watched Bella interacting with Tracey for a few minutes. Bella wasn't as free and easy as she was with Deepti, but she wasn't ignoring Tracey, which was an improvement from before.

Although Bella strongly resembled her mother, when she laughed she was the spitting image of his brother. He couldn't help remember the two of them as young boys, playing with and splashing each other in the pools when they'd been on holiday. They had been so close once upon a time, spending as much time as they could together, even after his brother had left home for university. But his brother's actions had ripped them apart.

'Did you want something?' Deepti asked, drawing his attention back to her.

'I was hoping to spend some time with Bella.'

'Now?' Deepti's eyes widened but she quickly recovered from her surprise that Matteo wanted to spend time with Bella during the day. 'She's been in the pool for a while, so she could be ready to come out now, but I wouldn't count on it. Your niece is definitely a water baby.'

'I'm not in a hurry,' he said, taking the lounger next to her.

'You could always get changed and join them.' Something in her tone made him look at her expression. What did that smile mean? Did she want to see him in swimming trunks?

He was already having a hard enough time not staring at Deepti in her bikini. He swallowed at the idea she might be attracted to him and wanted to see him bare-chested. Perhaps a cool dip in the pool was what he needed right now.

'Uncle Mayo!' Bella called, running over and throwing cold, wet arms around him. It was the first time she'd been physically affectionate to him and a lump formed in his throat.

'Hello, Bella,' he said, a little stiltedly. 'I came

to see if you wanted to play something or watch your pet programme.'

Bella nodded shyly.

'I should get Bella dry and dressed first,' Deepti said, gathering Leo up, ready to hand him to Tracey.

They all went back inside.

While Deepti was helping Bella wash and change, Matteo went to look at the cupboards surrounding the fridge, and thankfully found a coffee machine. He brewed a pot and put the carafe on a tray with cups, cream and sugar, remembering at the last minute to add a third cup for Tracey.

Tracey came into the living room first. 'Leo's down for his nap. Since Deepti's been staying with Bella, I've been going to the crew mess while he's sleeping, but if you want me to stay here…?'

Matteo shook his head. 'Not at all.'

He was more than happy to be alone with Deepti and Bella.

After spending almost an hour with Bella, Matteo needed to return to work. For the first time in a long time, the pull of the challenge and excitement of work wasn't as strong as the fun he'd been having with Deepti and Bella. 'Deepti, perhaps you can come to see me once Bella has gone to sleep?'

He felt a momentary pang of guilt at her look of alarm as she asked if there was a problem. Nobody wanted to do a bad job, but Deepti's reactions translated into a fear, which suggested she'd had previous experience that made her worry more than most people about her performance.

'Not at all,' he replied. 'We should have a catchup about how things are going with Bella. It's difficult to talk properly when she's around—unless Tracey has the evening off again?'

'No, she doesn't. I'll see you later.'

Later that evening, Matteo turned off his computer and leaned back in his chair, crossing his legs and putting his hands behind his head. Despite taking time out of his day to spend with Bella, he had accomplished everything he needed to, and it wasn't even eight o'clock. When he was working in his offices, it was rare that he finished work before ten. Between his executive assistant in London and his assistant on the yacht triaging anything that needed to be brought to Matteo's attention, work was being efficiently delegated, and he was the one benefiting most.

He heard a light knock before Deepti entered the room.

'Sorry, there was nobody in the front office. I didn't know whether you were still working or not. Bella's sleeping; is this a good time for you or I can come back when it's more convenient?'

He stood up. 'Perfect timing. I've just finished.'

He strode towards the lounge which gave access to the owner's suite. Deepti followed him as he walked over to the small dining room with a round table set for two.

'I was about to have dinner.'

She looked confused 'Oh, okay. I can come back in an hour or two, then.'

'Have you eaten?'

'Not yet.'

'Why don't you join me?' He reached the small dining table. 'There's plenty of food.'

'I can eat after we talk.'

He smiled. 'I told Chef you would be joining me.'

She still hesitated. Was it because she didn't want to eat with the boss or because of him personally?

'You'd be eating the same thing in the crew's mess,' he pointed out. 'What difference does the location make? We can talk while we eat so it's a working dinner.'

'Of course; that would be more efficient.' She sat down.

'Is red wine okay for you?' At her nod, he opened a bottle to let it breathe.

As he took the seat opposite her, she gave him an expectant look.

'So, do you have any specific questions about Bella?' she asked.

Matteo cleared his throat. He didn't have any questions about Bella. He could see for himself how she was improving. But he'd enjoyed talking with Deepti the previous evening and wouldn't mind her company again.

If he'd been on land and needed some company, he would have invited one of the many women who showed their interest in him out for a meal or to attend an exhibition or show. But he wasn't asking Deepti to dine with him as a substitute date. Although, he did admit, there was something about her that made him want to know her better, something more than looking at a beautiful face.

He caught her questioning look. 'Do you think Bella is settling down more?'

Deepti frowned. 'She seems fine to me. Quiet… but happy to play. Loves to swim. She's talking more to Tracey and seems happy for Tracey to help with washing and brushing.'

'That's good.'

'But I honestly don't have any experience of children. Bella talks about the nursery she used to go to for some mornings, and her friends, but she rarely talks about her parents or what she did with them. I don't know if that's unusual. And I don't know whether I should be bringing it up. I mean, you hardly mention your brother. If it's difficult for you to talk about him, it must be for Bella too.'

Matteo pressed his lips together tightly. 'My brother and I weren't close in recent years,' he said in clipped tones. 'In fact, I hadn't seen him since before Bella was born.'

He watched an interplay of expressions on Deepti's face but she said nothing, just carried on eating her steak and potatoes. He admired her restraint. It was unusual for him to bring it up at all, knowing that it would invite questions. But he felt an inexplicable compulsion to talk to Deepti about his family.

Every day, they got closer to Singapore and the moment he would see his parents again. His shoulders tightened. He honestly didn't know how he would react when he saw them. He couldn't understand the choice they'd made, which made a close relationship with them again unlikely.

'Would you like some dessert?' he asked.

'Sure.' When he gave her a plate but didn't

take any for himself, she asked, 'Aren't you having any?'

'I don't really eat a lot of sweet food. Is it good?'

She shrugged. 'Well, I like it. But it sounds immodest to say it's good when I made it.'

'You made it? Why are you working in the galley?'

'I'm not really but I asked Al… um…the chef if I could make the desserts for the crew occasionally even though my main role is to be with Bella. I know you didn't want dessert unless you had guests, so maybe I shouldn't have made them for the crew if you're not going to eat them. I can mention it to Alex.'

Again, there was the undue nervousness about whether she'd done something wrong.

'I don't want to deprive the crew of desserts,' he said. 'And, since you made this, I'll have to try some now.' He took a mouthful then practically moaned as the food melted on his tongue. It was amazing. Among the best desserts he'd ever tasted.

He loved sweet foods, perhaps a little too much, so he tried to eat them in moderation. But knowing Deepti was talented enough to make such exquisite food was going to make it difficult to keep to his resolve.

'This tastes like it was created by angels,' he said.

'Thank you!' Deepti's face brightened at his praise, making him think of sunlight again.

'Your *cordon bleu* qualification is well deserved. Did you work as a pastry chef in restaurants? Where did you say you live in England?'

'Um… London.' Deepti's voice was higher pitched that usual. He couldn't work out what about his question had unnerved her.

'I haven't worked as a pastry chef before,' she said.

'I see. Were you a sous chef?'

Her smile this time was forced. 'No. Actually, that reminds me, I need to speak to Alex.' She stood up. 'Goodnight.'

She hurried off before he could say anything. Matteo narrowed his eyes. Why was she being so evasive about working in a restaurant kitchen? Hiring decisions were left to the captain and heads of department, and he trusted them to do all the relevant background checks. There shouldn't have been any reason for her to be nervous about his questions.

Had his instinct on the first day been correct? Was there another reason Deepti had taken a job on *Serendipity* and got close to Bella?

And why did he hope he was wrong?

# CHAPTER SEVEN

DEEPTI HAD SPENT a lovely morning wandering around the small Italian town of Fiore. Walking down the narrow, cobblestone streets and looking at the mediaeval architecture, she felt as if she were in an EM Forster novel. Like most of the crew, she'd been surprised when Matteo had opted to anchor out at sea, and take the tender to Fiore rather than dock in one of Italy's bigger ports, but it was an unexpected treat.

And now she was getting hungry. The only difficulty was choosing which of the amazing restaurants to eat at.

'Deepti.'

Her heart leapt at the deep, gravelly voice she would recognise anywhere now. Had it really only been a week since she'd met Matteo?

'Matteo. I didn't expect to see you here. I thought you said your business was in the city.' They'd spoken briefly that morning when they'd travelled together to shore on the tender from the yacht but other members of the crew had been present so it had been a brief conversation.

'It was. My meetings are finished. I always come for a visit when I get the chance. My grandmother grew up in this town.'

'Oh, that's why we stopped here. I did wonder why you didn't choose one of the larger Italian harbours.'

He didn't make any comment but asked where Bella was.

'She's with Tracey. I think they've come to town but I haven't been with them this morning. It's my day off, so I thought I'd spend it exploring, and I can't expect a five-year-old to want to walk for hours. It feels like ages since I've been on land. It's funny how quickly you can get used to being at sea.'

He inclined his head in agreement. 'Have you been to Italy before?'

'Oh, yes, plenty of times. My mum loves Italy. We used to go all the time when I was in high school. But we always stayed near the main tourist areas.'

'Where are you about to go now?'

Deepti looked around her. 'Actually, I was going to find somewhere to eat. Can you recommend a place? They all look amazing to me.'

For a moment, Matteo said nothing but stood staring at her. He had that same inscrutable expression. Would she ever know what he was thinking? It was a strange dichotomy, knowing he was such a frank and open person in some ways.

This was completely unlike her. She was lying to him every day, or at least hiding the truth. But she couldn't give up the enjoyment of spending time with someone who didn't know the truth about her job; someone who wasn't going to judge her or believe she was at best unethical and at worst a criminal.

'Never mind,' she said when he still didn't reply. 'I'm sure all of them will be great. I'll see you back on the boat.' She started to walk towards the tavernas.

'Just wait.' Matteo put a detaining hand on her arm. 'I'm taking a break for lunch. I have a reservation. It's a bit of a trek, but well worth it.'

'Oh, is it quite popular, then? Do you think I'll be able to get a table?'

Matteo rolled his eyes. 'Yes. Because I'm asking you to join me.'

'Oh, no, I don't want to spoil your lunch break.'

'Not at all. I wouldn't mind the company.'

Deepti still hesitated. She wanted to spend time with Matteo, and that was concerning. It had only been a month since she'd broken up with her boyfriend and, although he had been far from the love of her life, she shouldn't be interested in someone new already, should she? She tried to reassure herself that wanting to spend some time with someone for interesting conversation was nothing to worry about, and definitely didn't mean she was looking for a relationship.

Perhaps it was her forced proximity to Matteo that was causing these unwelcome feelings of attraction. She really should refuse to join him. In fact, she should go out of her way to avoid spending much time alone with him. She stuck out her chin in a gesture of resolve.

'Deepti, please would you join me for lunch?' There was an almost pleading expression in his eyes.

'I would love to,' she replied, her resolve immediately disappearing. She mentally rolled her eyes at how pathetic she was acting.

They'd been walking for five minutes when Matteo suddenly stopped.

'As I said, it is a bit of a trek to get to the restaurant. We can either keep following the road round, or we can take this path, which is a shortcut.'

Deepti looked around, not really clear what path Matteo was referring to. Her nose crinkled.

Matteo laughed. 'All right, it's not really a path. It's a little overgrown.' He moved the branches of a large bush to the side to reveal a dirt track. 'It can be steep, so we can use the road is you prefer.'

'I don't mind the path, but won't your suit get muddy?'

'I don't have any meetings this afternoon. But I always keep a spare suit in all my offices.'

Deepti's lips quirked. He mentioned having multiple offices, no doubt in multiple countries, as if it was a usual occurrence. She was used to working with CEOs and CFOs of some major companies, but she suspected Matteo was in a different league entirely.

'Then lead the way,' she said, throwing her arm out in front of her.

Matteo had warned her the path wasn't easy, but that had been an understatement. He was solicitous of her, holding back branches to avoid her being scratched, but the uneven and stony ground, together with the steep incline, was tricky to navigate. She focused her attention on not tripping over.

Although Deepti knew Matteo was adjusting his speed to accommodate her, she still struggled to match his pace with the incline. Suddenly, he turned round and walked back over to her, holding out his hand.

'Here, let me help you—we're coming to the

hardest part now. But we should be there soon. I promise you that it will be worth it.'

The smile that he gave her made the difficulty of the path worth it. Without thinking, Deepti put out her hand, instantly feeling secure as it was enveloped by his larger one.

Finally, the path came out at a narrow road with a group of white stone houses in the shadow of fruit trees. The road had a view of the coast, and in the distance she could see *Serendipity* at anchor.

She began to let go of Matteo's hand but had to give it a tug to release it fully. Or had she imagined the resistance? She sneaked a look at Matteo.

He seemed startled. He cleared his throat. 'Right. It's that place over there.'

He strode across to one of the buildings which had some tables outside. The same large crowds that she seen on the street below were not gathered outside the restaurant, and there was no visible menu outside.

As soon as they set foot inside, Matteo was welcomed by an older lady with silver-streaked brown hair. Her greeting was warmer than Deepti would have expected if Matteo had been simply a regular returning customer; it was the kind given to a much-loved family member.

Matteo and the owner conversed in Italian

for a few moments before he turned to introduce Deepti.

'Welcome, Deepti,' the lady said, speaking in fluent English. 'Any friend of our Matteo is very welcome here. Are you happy to sit outside?'

Deepti smiled her agreement, recalling the amazing view as they'd come out of the bushes.

As they took their seats, Matteo explained there weren't any menus since the owners decided what to make based on what fresh produce they got in the mornings. 'Let them know if you have any dietary requirements, of course,' he said, 'But usually I trust their recommendations. They haven't let me down yet.'

'Okay.' She looked around at the view. 'It's so peaceful here. But out of the way. How did you find it?' she asked Matteo.

'My family have been coming here for years. The restaurant has been in the same ownership for generations.'

It was interesting how Matteo clearly felt a connection to this place, where his grandmother had grown up, and yet she got the impression there was something slightly frosty about his relationship with his parents. She wondered if she would ever know what was behind it.

'How lovely to have a genuine family business. You started your company, I understand?'

'That's right. There was no expectation for me

to follow in my family's footsteps, but a family business was a goal at one point. I did hope my bro—'

He broke off. 'What about you? Any chefs in your family?'

'No.' She examined her fingers so she wouldn't have to look at him. 'Both my parents are accountants so I guess I did follow—' She clamped her mouth tight before she revealed they all worked in the financial sector. She still didn't want Matteo to know she'd been fired. She'd already been judged by so many people she worked with, it was refreshing to talk to someone who didn't know about that part of her life, so they couldn't judge her on what had happened.

She'd noticed his suspicious look when she'd prevaricated about her job experience before she'd come on the boat. Hopefully, the worst he would think was that she'd got the job through her friendship with Alex and would not delve too deeply into it. It wasn't unusual for junior crew members, particularly assistant chefs, to have limited experience before taking on the role. It wasn't as if she was completely unqualified as a pastry chef.

And he hadn't cared that she was totally unqualified to be a care-giver to Bella. Although his phrasing it as her being Bella's companion meant the only qualification she needed for her role was for Bella to enjoy spending time with her.

He was quite different from the man she'd thought he was after their first meeting. She'd assumed he was cold and unapproachable, maintaining a clear distinction between himself as the owner of *Serendipity* and the crew. In fact, he was almost the exact opposite. W,henever he kept his distance from the crew she could tell it was because he didn't want to make them uncomfortable.

She'd made assumptions based on her experience of the people she'd met as part of her previous job. But, although Matteo was clearly a successful businessman, he was a good employer who cared for his staff and was kind and generous. It was as if his attitude to Bella, when they'd initially met, was the aberration.

But now he was adapting to Bella, the same way Deepti was, which made Deepti wonder again what the story was behind his attitude to his parents and brother. But she couldn't ask him for more details. And she couldn't expect him to be honest with her when she was being anything but honest with him.

Gradually their conversation turned from work to more personal topics. They talked about books again, which segued into a chat about how they spent their spare time. Deepti loved getting a chance to open up to him and have him reciprocate. But it took an intense effort to concentrate on making coherent responses when all she wanted to do was stare at the male perfection sitting across from her.

Shadows from the afternoon sun delineated the sharp cheekbones of his classically handsome face and drew her eyes to the full temptation of his lips. But it wasn't just his physical attributes. He was intelligent, witty and surprisingly charming. Exactly the kind of person she would want to date in any other circumstances. If they'd met in England, would he have invited her out? Once upon a time, she would have accepted without hesitation.

She immediately discarded that fanciful notion. They would never have met in England. It was only a quirk of fate that they were in each other's company at all. But for the first time in months, or perhaps even longer than that, she felt genuinely happy. She was exactly where she wanted to be.

Finally, they finished their meal. As Matteo paid, he said, 'I don't have any meetings until this evening. Would you like me to show you round this town some more?'

'I would love that!' Deepti replied, excited that she would get to be with Matteo for a little longer. Then it clicked that he probably wasn't suggesting an outing for the two of them alone. 'I'll text Tracey to ask her to meet us somewhere with Bella and Leo. Bella would love to spend time with you during the day.'

Matteo's expression was startled, then he blinked and said, 'Of course. We should head back down the hill, then.'

He put a guiding hand on the small of her back. Something intense flared through her at the simple gesture.

# CHAPTER EIGHT

MATTEO STRETCHED AND got up from his seat. It had been non-stop meetings since they'd set sail from Italy four days ago. Having most of his meetings by video conference, and only meeting in person when privacy or networking was the priority, had increased his efficiency tenfold. The decision to incorporate this floating office into his business practices was working out well.

From a work perspective, the whole sailing experience seemed to be working out well too. And his decision to ask Deepti to be Bella's companion was also working better than he'd expected. He'd enjoyed that brief time he'd spent with Deepti in Fiore, and he could see why Bella had formed at attachment to her.

Matteo forced himself to call Jack in so they could talk through the final arrangements for the next day's work. Once that was done, Matteo was effectively finished for the day. In the past he would have ploughed on—there were always more deals he could be working on.

Instead, he went out to his deck, where the dry heat of the Egyptian desert hit him immediately as the yacht began its slow, incredibly slow, passage through the Suez Canal towards Port Said.

He didn't have any in-person meetings scheduled for when they were in Cairo so he had initially planned to stay on *Serendipity* to work. But, with the amount of progress he'd made, he could take a day off to explore the city.

Matteo heard steps behind him. Without turning, he instinctively knew it was Deepti. How was he already so attuned to her?

'Sorry to disturb you,' she said. He stifled the ripple of awareness that went through him at the sound of her soft, low voice. 'Jack said it was okay for me to come through.'

Matteo looked at her and gave a brief nod, then turned back to his view. Deepti came to stand next to him, resting her hands on the rail. She sighed deeply.

'Is something wrong?' he asked.

'No. Not at all,' she replied, shaking her head slowly as she looked towards the banks. 'It's just so still. Not that the journey has been choppy at all, but the complete nothingness around us...' She shrugged. 'Sorry, ignore me. I came to give you an update on Bella, since it's my evening off.'

They'd continued their daily updates whenever he wasn't entertaining guests in the evenings, even though he could see for himself that Bella was enjoying her time with Deepti and was much happier in herself. He found himself looking forward to their catch-ups.

It turned out Deepti was just as much a companion for him as she was for Bella. On future trips on *Serendipity*, he would need to think about bringing someone along for company, although he couldn't imagine not getting bored with them in a way that hadn't happened with Deepti.

'Do you have anything planned for the evening?' he asked when she'd finished her update. He turned round so he could face her and leaned back, resting his elbows on the railing.

'Nothing specific.' She quickly removed her hands from the rails and straightened but continued to stare straight ahead.

He waited for her to tell him more about her plans and was surprised when she remained silent. It wasn't unusual for them to chat generally after they'd finished talking about Bella. They often shared a bottle of wine as they discussed current events, literature, the arts or sport. Deepti was an interesting and thought-provoking conversationalist.

On a couple of occasions he had found himself wanting to get her opinion on some work ideas he had—and he had never wanted to share that part of his life with people outside the business—but Deepti actively changed the subject when he mentioned business. He didn't expect her to have subject knowledge of the world of finance, he just wanted to get her common-sense thoughts.

Even though they'd barely known each other a week when they'd had lunch together in Fiore, it had felt like a date. He had even been tempted to tell Deepti about his estrangement from his family—to explain, perhaps justify, why he wasn't close to Bella and Leo.

What was it about her that made him feel he could trust her with his story? There was something calming about her; he felt relaxed when they talked—as relaxed as he could be when his body went onto high alert whenever there was any contact between them. And the attraction was growing, perhaps because of the way he felt when they talked.

Being attracted to Deepti, opening up to her, was unexpected…and unwelcome. He didn't want to open himself up to any woman. Not when the evidence of his greatest betrayal was travelling with him to Singapore.

He pressed his lips together. He couldn't really see Bella that way. She was an innocent child and in no way responsible for the actions of her parents. He almost regretted that he hadn't had a relationship with his niece and nephew before their trip.

When Bella and Leo had joined Deepti and him in Fiore, he hadn't anticipated how bittersweet it would be to show the children some of the places their father had played as a child. Memories had rushed in of the times when the two brothers had been so close; when he'd believed nothing, and no one, could come between them and break their bond. Or perhaps the distance had started before then and he just hadn't noticed. He had been so busy trying to establish his business, he'd been oblivious to many things.

The residual anger he usually experienced when he thought about his ex-fiancée with his brother didn't come this time. Instead, he felt sorrow. He knew now that his ex-fiancée hadn't been the right person for him, but it had taken too long for him to learn that. He'd only known Deepti a week and he felt a stronger connection to her than he'd ever felt to the woman he'd thought he'd marry. But the lasting legacy of his fiancée's betrayal meant he would never be able to trust someone enough to enter into a real, emotional relationship with them.

Deepti pressed her hand on his but didn't

try to break the silence that had fallen between them—a small gesture but indicative of how empathetic he'd come to know Deepti to be. The warmth of her hand echoed a similar warmth growing in the region of his chest.

'Anyway, I'll leave you in peace,' she said, about to walk away.

Instinctively, he reached out and grasped her wrist.

'You haven't seen the library yet, have you?' he asked. 'If you don't have any plans now, why don't I show you?'

She opened her mouth then closed it again and simply nodded. He smothered a grin. He could tell she'd been about to tell him she could find the library herself if he gave her directions—it was her default response. He wasn't sure whether it was because she thought he was too busy to spend time with her or whether there was another reason.

He led her out of the lounge, across the foyer. To the left was his bedroom, but he purposefully ignored the temptation to take Deepti in there, and went to the room opposite instead.

'Ta dah!' he said as he walked into the library and swept his arm out. The room was wall-to-wall bookcases extending to the ceiling. There was a rail running across the length of one of the shelves for a ladder to slide across.

'Wow!' Deepti laughed reverentially. 'I feel like I just stepped into a fairy tale.'

'What?'

She was walking next to the shelves, running a hand across the books, occasionally selecting one and pulling it to read the back cover.

'Oh,' she said. 'There was just a scene like this in an animated film I watched with Bella, appropriately.'

He blinked, giving her a blank look.

'The character had a similar name,' she explained.

'I see,' he said, not sure he really did.

Deepti giggled. 'We really have to diversify your taste in movies. I feel like you're missing out a lot.'

He quirked an eyebrow. 'Really?'

'Trust me,' she replied with a cheeky grin.

His smile fell. It was such an innocuous phrase—'trust me'—but something he found hard to do, particularly when it came to attractive women. How was he supposed to trust anyone when the woman he'd been supposed to marry had betrayed his trust so indelibly?

Since that time, he had never let any woman get close to him. In a matter of weeks, Deepti had slipped past his first line of defence. Perhaps it was because there weren't many people on board he could, or wanted to, spend his free time with. He needed to restrict how often he was alone with her.

He'd been about to ask Deepti to join him for a drink once they'd finished in the library but he changed his mind.

'I'll leave you to enjoy the library,' he said, deliberately ignoring the disappointment on her face.

He couldn't allow Deepti to get closer to him. She wasn't a colleague and, even though he wasn't technically her direct employer in her new role, while she was on the yacht, she was under his overall charge, like all staff and crew. In other circumstances, she could have been a friend but, whatever she was, she was totally out of bounds.

Two days later, Deepti was sitting out on the main deck reading while *Serendipity* was moored in Port Said. The majority of the crew, including Deepti, were being given time off while they were in Egypt. The previous day, she'd gone with Alex, his girlfriend and the replacement assistant chef for a quick trip around the port.

That morning, since Tracey was still working, Deepti had offered to help her out. Although they'd only been on the boat for a couple of weeks, Bella had already warmed to Tracey. But she'd still been surprised when Tracey had turned her down, explaining that she was worried that Matteo's parents would think she was incompetent if she couldn't look after the two children on her own.

Watching Bella happily leave the yacht without her that morning, Deepti reflected that, at this rate, she was the one who probably wouldn't be needed soon.

When she found out Matteo had arranged to meet Bella and Leo to be their guide around Cairo, she was relieved Tracey had refused her offer. Part of Deepti desperately wanted to explore with them but, even though Tracey urged her to join them at the time, she came up with an excuse. It didn't seem wise to join them when she was thinking about Matteo so much.

She hadn't seen Matteo since the night he'd showed her the library—not to speak to, anyway. For the last couple of days, she'd taken an early-morning swim in the outside pool. She was convinced Matteo had been exercising in the gym below. She didn't know for sure that it was him, but her instinct had said it was, and it gave her a sense of connection that the two of them were alone, together, out there.

And that feeling was alarming.

She missed him and it had barely been forty-eight hours. She had to be sensible. He was spending time with Bella and Leo, not with her. And their evening catch-ups were about the children. Although lately they'd spent most of their time together discussing anything and everything else.

Maybe she was enjoying adult conversation rather than Matteo himself. She discarded that reason immediately. She got plenty of adult conversation with Tracey, Alex and the other crew members.

There was no explanation for why she liked being with Matteo—apart from his amazing looks. Perhaps she really was just that shallow. Deepti laughed to herself. She'd taken loads of pictures of Matteo and the children and might have sneaked a surreptitious photo of Matteo on his own. If his looks were all she cared about, she could stare at a photo.

She wasn't the only person on the yacht who appreciated Matteo's face and physique. He was a regular topic of conversation in the crew mess. If only Deepti could take a leaf out of Tracey's book. Tracey was completely unaffected by Matteo.

What was wrong with her? Less than two months ago, she'd been in a relationship with someone else. Granted, her feelings for her ex had been lukewarm at best, but she had trusted him.

How naive she'd been. Not only had his attachment been a pretence, but he'd obviously done something to get the deal she was after which had led to the client being lost. She wasn't a believer in coincidences. If she could be with someone for almost a year and not really know them, how could she trust her judgement about anything, or anyone, else?

'Why do I suspect your thoughts are worth more than a penny?' Matteo's deep voice caused Deepti to jump, making her book fall off her lap.

Matteo walked forward, picked it up then he glanced at the cover and frowned.

She grabbed the book out of his hands. It wasn't one of her usual reads, being a non-fiction book about finance which she'd seen in the library. Luckily, it would be difficult for Matteo to comment on her choice without coming across as judgemental, but she wanted to avoid any risk he would talk about it.

'I didn't realise you were back,' Deepti said.

'It was getting too hot for the children.'

She wanted to snatch off the linen bucket-hat he was wearing, to release his wavy hair, but it suited him so ridiculously well. Her eyes raked over the rest of him, down his navy-blue T-shirt stretched tightly against his broad chest to his strong, tanned arms and lower... Her mouth went dry—Matteo in cargo shorts which stopped just below his knees was a sight to behold. She had never thought of muscular calves as particularly sexy before but her body's reaction, every nerve-ending taut and on edge, told her differently. She needed to get away.

'Okay. I'll go to Bella now,' she said.

'No need,' he replied. 'Tracey's trying to get both of them down for a nap. And it's your day off.'

'But I have nothing planned, so I don't mind.'

Matteo frowned. 'I thought you had something on.'

She had initially intended to spend her time exploring Cairo, but having an empty boat had also been a good opportunity to catch up on emails and start thinking about her work situation—there were only a few weeks left before she would be heading back to England—but it had been too disheartening and she'd chosen to read instead.

'I decided I was too lazy to go ashore,' she replied.

The look he gave her was sceptical. She didn't blame him. Who would be too lazy to explore Cairo? 'I've been to Egypt before.'

'You didn't mention you've been to Cairo before,' he said, furrowing his brow.

'Giza. But it's all the same, isn't it?' Deepti closed her eyes tight with mortification as he looked taken aback. She really was bad at prevaricating. 'Anyway, I think I'll go and wash the heat off me.'

She went back to her room and sat on the bed. She had to get her body under control. Her intense attraction to Matteo was inappropriate. What she felt wasn't real. She could trust her emotions.

# CHAPTER NINE

THERE WAS NO one around in the children's play areas or bedrooms when Matteo was finally free to visit. He'd had business guests for the last week, which meant he hadn't been able to spend time with Bella.

He was surprised by the fact he'd missed her. The little five-year-old girl was worming her way into his heart. And her brother was exceptionally cute too.

And it had been too long since he'd chatted with Deepti. He should have suggested continuing their catch-ups even when he had guests on board. He missed their chats.

He wondered whether it was solely due to enjoying the company of a beautiful woman. She wasn't like the women he typically dated. Even so, if they'd met under different circumstances, he would have asked her out. But that would have been a bad idea, because he rarely dated the same woman for more than a few weeks—

he would have missed out on getting to know Deepti better if he had opted for a couple of nights in her bed.

Concerned at the direction of his thoughts, he left the children's living room and crossed the lobby to the port-side state rooms. He tried calling Deepti's and Tracey's phones but his calls went to voicemail.

He went down to the lower deck in case they were in the beach club. As he was walking past the gym, the door to the cinema room opened and Deepti walked out.

'Oh, hello,' she said. His face brightened at the sight of her smile. 'I saw you'd rung, so came out to see what you wanted.'

'I was looking for Bella. She's not in her room.'

'Oh, no, we're in here. We've watched a few episodes of *Pets in Petland* and were about to start a film. But I can bring her out.'

'No, that's fine, I can join you.'

They walked into the cinema room. The seating was arranged on three levels with two large body-length sofas on each level. Each sofa arm had a cup-holder and tray for a snack. Bella was curled up on a sofa at the back. A carelessly folded throw next to her indicated Deepti had been sitting next to her.

'Deepti,' Tracey said, while she lifted a sleepy

Leo in her arms. 'I'm going to put this little one down for the night. I'll come back in an hour for Bella.'

'Oh, I can take her back.'

Tracey cast Matteo a look. 'No, that's fine. I'll see you in a bit.'

'Uncle Mayo. Come sit here!' Bella called enthusiastically, patting the sofa next to her.

'Okay, princess,' he said. He sat down, then took his shoes off so he could stretch out his legs. 'What are we going to watch?'

'We have the cartoons you downloaded for her the last time we docked,' Deepti said. 'Or there's a film with talking animals, or one with talking tools, or one with talking cars.' Deepti bit her lip as she tried not to smile. Her expression told him that she wasn't particularly looking forward to the films.

'Animals,' Bella said.

As Deepti loaded the film, she looked over Bella's head at Matteo and whispered, 'Escape now. You really don't have to put yourself through this.'

Matteo grinned. He shook his head and settled back on the sofa. Bella nestled closer to him. He put his arm around her, bringing her in for a cuddle, and pressed a soft kiss against the top of her head. If someone had told him, even two months ago, that he would choose to watch a children's movie instead of working, he would have laughed at them. But now he wanted to spend more time with this sweet child and her brother before they had to part in Singapore. He hugged Bella again at the unexpected twinge of sadness that he wouldn't see her as much in the future.

He was sure his parents would be wonderful guardians for Bella and Leo, and it was in the children's best interests to stay with them. His parents might not have supported him over his brother, they might have disappointed him and they might not have been there for him, but he knew they loved their grandchildren. He knew they had visited Bella and Leo in England every few months, and his mother had stayed with them for over a month to help out when Leo had been born. He knew because his parents had sent him a message each time they were in England, wanting him to meet up with them—messages he always ignored.

'Uncle Mayo, look there,' Bella said, bouncing up and down while pointing to the screen. He turned his attention back to the film.

Bella made it through almost fifty minutes before falling asleep. Deepti paused the film and stood up.

'I'll take her to her room.'

'I can do that,' Matteo replied, whispering back.

Deepti opened her mouth, no doubt to argue with him, but they were interrupted by Tracey, who'd returned to collect Bella, as she'd told them she would.

Once they were alone, Deepti seemed nervous.

'I'll clear all this away,' she said, pointing to the snacks and blankets.

He caught her look over at the screen where they'd paused the film.

He narrowed his eyes. 'You're going to finish watching it, aren't you?' he asked, his lips quirking.

Deepti giggled. 'I'm quite invested in it now. I'm not sure I can wait until Bella's ready to watch it again.' She gave him an embarrassed shrug.

Without replying, he sat back on the sofa and indicated she should press play.

'Really, you're going to watch it too?' Her look was sceptical.

'What can I say? I want to find out how it ends. And I may not be there when Bella finishes it.'

'I guess, if you don't have anything better to do.'

Matteo looked at Deepti intently, not sure why he didn't leave. He had a thousand things he could be doing instead—there was always work to do—or he could watch a film suitable for adults, or he could read. But, at that moment in time, none of the options sounded *better* than spending his evening next to Deepti, even when they were watching a kids' programme.

He turned to the screen and said slightly curtly, 'Let's start.'

Slowly, and without being consciously aware, as they watched he moved closer to Deepti on the couch. Or had she moved too? He was resting his arm along the back of the couch and Deepti was leaning back, almost touching him. The temptation to move his arm slightly so it dropped across Deepti's shoulders was powerful.

He didn't know if the gesture would be welcome. He wasn't sure whether it was appropriate, even though he wasn't technically her employer. That thought was enough for him to abruptly move his arm off the back of the sofa.

As far as he could recall, Deepti had initially only signed up to crew until they reached Singapore, which had worked perfectly with the change of her role to that of Bella's companion. He had no idea what her plans were after they reached their destination.

Deepti sighed, bringing his attention back to his surroundings. The film had ended.

'What are you doing after we get to Singapore? he asked.

Deepti looked at him in surprise. He supposed the question had come out of nowhere.

'I'll probably fly back to England.'

'You're not staying to crew on the yacht?' That was good news.

'No. This was only temporary.'

'What will you do back in England?'

'Look for another job.' She smiled but she didn't hold his gaze. Again, it was quite clear that she was withholding something from him. Rather than pursue that line of questioning, he asked her about her plans for the next few days instead—so he knew when he could spend time with Bella.

Although it had started as a condition to get Deepti to take on the role of companion, the time he spent with them was one of the highlights of his day. He would miss them once they got to Singapore.

Deepti looked as though she was getting ready to leave.

'It's still early. Why don't we watch another movie?' he suggested. 'We could even look for something that doesn't feature talking inanimate objects or animals.'

Deepti hesitated for a moment. Then, taking a noticeable breath, she said. 'Sure. Why don't you choose? Anything but horror.'

That was a shame. Horrors were the perfect films to use to get up close to someone. He scanned through the available options.

'How about a thriller, then?' he suggested. 'You love reading them. Do you like watching them too?'

'I do,' she said, with a slightly surprised but happy expression.

Why did she seem pleased he'd remembered what genre she enjoyed? He would have remembered that about anyone. His eyes widened at the realisation that that wasn't true. It was the kind of detail he didn't bother noting most of the time, let alone recalling. So why did he know so much about Deepti?

'Matteo…' Deepti's voice broke into his thoughts.

'Hmm?'

'I said the film's ready.' She tilted her head. 'Is everything okay?'

No, everything wasn't okay. He was unsure of himself, which made him uncomfortable. There had to be a simple explanation for his growing interest in Deepti but, until he worked out what it was, the best thing for him to do would be to find an excuse to leave.

She was still watching him intently, a curious half-smile playing on her lips. He sighed deeply—she was so beautiful. He was only watching a film with her, after all. There was nothing to worry about with that activity. They could maintain their distance even if they shared the couch.

'Ready when you are,' he said.

They both leant back on the sofa. Within minutes, instead of keeping his distance, Matteo spread a throw over both of them.

It took a Herculean effort to resist holding Deepti, particularly when he heard her gasps and quickening breath when something unexpected happened on screen.

When the film finished, Deepti lifted her face to look at him.

'That was so good!' she exclaimed. 'I never expected that. Did you?'

Matteo shook his head. If he'd been paying full attention to the film, he probably would have seen the signs, but he'd spent as much time watching the varied expressions cross Deepti's face as he had watching the film itself. He felt he knew exactly what had happened based on her expression.

She was still looking up at him, the light from the screen playing across her delicate facial bones. He slowly started to bend his head.

A noise from the door snagged his attention.

'Oh, sorry, Mr Di Corrado, I didn't realise you were still in here,' a crew member said. 'I was just doing my rounds to check everything is in order.'

'Everything's fine,' Matteo replied, watching Deepti hastily pick up her stuff and leave the room.

He grimaced. Could she tell he'd been about to kiss her? And was she as disappointed by the interruption as he was?

# CHAPTER TEN

THE NEXT DAY, Deepti had the afternoon off to explore Abu Dhabi. She, Matteo, Tracey and the children had disembarked from *Serendipity* when it had docked that morning and gone straight to the hotel they were staying at instead of sleeping on the yacht. After accompanying them to their suite, Matteo had gone to his first business meeting.

Once they'd freshened up in the hotel, Tracey asked Deepti to leave her alone with the children, and they would all meet up again for lunch.

Deepti decided to visit Capital Gate. Although she tried to absorb the skyscraper's unique leaning design and intricate diagrid architecture, it was difficult when she was alone with her thoughts. And she couldn't help replaying what had happened in the cinema room the previous evening.

Had he really been about to kiss her? He'd been staring at her intently. But perhaps she'd had popcorn on her face, or her eyeliner had smudged, or he was going to remove an eyelash. There were hundreds of reasons he could have been looking at her. And perhaps he'd been moving his head to get a better look.

Thank goodness she hadn't given in to her urge to stand on tiptoes to bring his head even closer. She would never know what would have happened if they hadn't been interrupted. But she should be grateful they had been. Her life was already too complicated.

When she finally arrived at the restaurant for lunch, she was surprised to see that Matteo had joined them. As they ate, Bella told them about her morning. Occasionally Deepti would meet Matteo's gaze and smile, affectionate, contented smiles because of Bella. Who would have thought that this little chatterbox at the table had barely spoken to anyone when their journey had started?

Once they had finished eating, Tracey had told them she was taking the children back to the hotel.

'Mr Di Corrado, since you said you don't have any afternoon meetings, why don't you show Deepti around? She hasn't been here before.'

'Oh, that's not necessary,' Deepti replied hurriedly.

'Happy to,' Matteo said at the same time.

'Okay, I guess,' Deepti said, giving Tracey an assessing look. Tracey couldn't possibly be match-making, could she?

'I have to make a quick call,' Matteo said. 'But we can go after that.'

'Tracey, what are you up to?' Deepti asked when Matteo had moved away to make his call.

'I don't know what you mean,' Tracey replied with an innocent expression. But she couldn't help a mischievous smile.

'Why are you trying to make Matteo spend time with me?'

'Am I?' Tracey's high-pitched voice betrayed her.

'Tracey, you can't possibly think something's going to happen between me and Matteo?'

Tracey shrugged. 'I think Mr Di Corrado could do with relaxing more. He enjoys spending time with you. You can help him relax.'

Deepti narrowed her eyes. 'I didn't realise you know Matteo so well.'

'I don't. Not as well as you. But then, he's never asked me to call him Matteo.' Tracey raised her eyebrows as if she was making a meaningful point. Deepti sighed. Why did people keep bringing up the name thing?

'Anyway,' Tracey continued, 'It's all sorted now. I'll see you back at the hotel.'

'If—'

'Don't worry—I will call if there are any problems. Enjoy yourself.' She waggled her fingers then she helped Bella onto the buggy board behind the pram and walked off.

Deepti stared after her, shaking her head. The last thing she needed was a matchmaker. Perhaps she should make it clear to Tracey she wasn't interested in any kind of romantic entanglement—not even with someone as gorgeous as Matteo.

'Have the others left?' Matteo asked when he came back to their table.

'Yes, just a few minutes ago. Shall we go?' she asked, heading towards the exit.

'Is there anywhere particular you want to go first?' he asked when they were standing outside the restaurant.

Deepti shook her head. She could sense Matteo looking at her but she didn't turn her head. She was stiff and awkward, trying not to think about the previous night or what Tracey had said. And standing so close to him wasn't helping the whirl of confusion in her head.

'Would you like to go shopping or to a museum?'

'Actually, I think I might join some of the crew for a few hours.'

'Sure—where are you meeting them? I'll walk you there.'

Of course, since Deepti had only just come up with that idea, she had nowhere to suggest.

'I'm still waiting for Alex to text me the details.' She glanced at him briefly, catching his puzzled expression. As a naturally honest person, it wasn't surprising she was so bad at lying but now, instead of trying to deflect attention from herself, she'd probably increased it.

'I see. I'll walk with you until you hear back from him. The Heritage Village is very close to here, or there's a mall too. Why don't we head in that direction until you hear from Alex?'

They walked in silence for a while. For the first time since she'd taken on the role of Bella's companion, she felt uncomfortable.

She wasn't a fool. She knew she and Matteo had been getting closer; it was probably inevitable with the amount of time they'd spent together. And she had obviously always known he was an attractive man. That was simply an objective fact. But she hadn't really believed that he was attracted to her too. And a one-sided attraction was relatively safe because it wouldn't go anywhere.

Rationally, if he had tried to kiss her in the cinema room, he would have addressed it in some way, wouldn't he? It must have been her imagination, or at most wishful thinking.

'What's wishful thinking?' Matteo asked.

Deepti closed her eyes, cringing at the realisation she'd spoken out loud. Hopefully, it was only the last part he'd heard. She quickly cast around in her mind for a credible response. 'Oh, living somewhere like this permanently.'

'Of all the places you've visited, you want to live in Abu Dhabi?' He raised an eyebrow.

'Maybe not here specifically, but somewhere with warm weather.' She mentally rolled her eyes as she came up with that excuse. 'What about you?' she asked, trying to deflect the attention from herself. 'You can live anywhere. Why do you have your main base in London and not Singapore, since you have family there? Or you could have chosen Tokyo or even New York, Paris or Frankfurt. I would love to live in any one of those cities if I had the choice.'

'I have ties in London.' He shrugged. They walked together in silence for a few minutes until he stopped and turned to her, asking, 'Do you know much about finance?'

'Why do you ask that?' She avoided his gaze, feigning an interest in one of the buildings they were passing.

'You were reading a book on it the other day and you just named the main financial cities. Not many people outside finance would know them.'

'Oh, I'm excellent at general knowledge quizzes,' she replied with absolute truth.

'Really? Me too. There are some great places for pub-type quizzes here. Perhaps we should go tonight.' Her heart flipped as his excited grin made the corners of his eyes crinkle.

'That would be fantastic! I bet some of the crew would love to go to.'

Matteo's smile fell but he hurriedly said, 'Of course. If Tracey wants to go, I can also organise a babysitter in the hotel. Let me make a couple of calls.'

Deepti walked away from him to gather her thoughts. Matteo was a gorgeous man, and not just in terms of his looks. It was only natural that she would be attracted to him. It made perfect sense that she was falling for him.

But he was out of her league, not that she was looking for a relationship. After what had happened with her ex, she doubted she would ever trust her own judgement about men.

What did she really know about Matteo? He was kind, he was caring, he was attentive, he was passionate—she knew that much. Or maybe she was wrong about that. Although she didn't think she was. But it didn't matter. A relationship with Matteo wasn't possible. Which was fine, because she didn't want one.

She groaned inwardly, trying to control her

overactive brain from obsessing over something that was never going to happen.

When she'd stayed on board *Serendipity* while the others had toured Cairo, she'd given into her curiosity and done an Internet search on Matteo. And some of the sites she'd found—particularly those which loved to dish the dirt on the love lives of the rich and famous—suggested he didn't have long-term relationships. He was often referred to as a commitment-phobe.

Having a relationship with Matteo would be a fantasy on so many levels. She wasn't free to indulge in a romance—not when her life was so complicated. She needed to sort herself out before she could move forward.

No matter how far away her troubles seemed when she was walking along the beach in Abu Dhabi, they would still be there waiting for her when she got back to England. Tempting as it was to draw a line behind her and look for work in a different field, she couldn't let her name and the reputation she'd built up just disappear.

She jumped when a hand touched her shoulder.

'I'm sorry,' Matteo said. 'I didn't mean to startle you. You were miles away. You didn't answer when I called your name.' He turned her to face him and put both hands on her shoulder, staring at her intently. 'Are you sure everything's okay? You seem to have a lot on your mind.'

'I guess I do.'

'Anything I can help you with?'

Ironically, if she could have told Matteo the truth, he probably would have been able to help her with his expertise. But she still couldn't bring herself to admit her past failure. And what if he didn't believe that she had acted innocently, but thought that she was actually guilty of what she'd been fired for? She didn't know how she would feel if he wasn't on her side and, despite only knowing him for a short time, she valued getting to know him and wanted him to have a good opinion of her.

There were only a few weeks now until they reached Singapore. She would cherish the time she got to spend with him and protect her heart.

'It's nothing important. I'm realising how close we are to Singapore. Getting to crew on this yacht is a once-in-a-lifetime opportunity. I can't believe it will end soon. But I'm going to soak up every second until then.'

She lifted her face to the sun and closed her eyes. After a couple of seconds, she realised how ridiculous she must look and hurriedly dropped her head and opened her eyes.

Matteo was standing next to her, his head facing up to the sun with his eyes closed, a small smile playing on his lips.

Deepti sighed deeply. Her heart was already in so much trouble.

Later that evening, Matteo and Deepti were in a sports pub listening intently to the questions, as the quiz was getting to a crucial stage. The competition was really between two teams, one of which was his. Although Alex, the head steward and two other crew members had joined them at the pub to form a team, it had really been a two-person show with Deepti and him.

Thank goodness he'd agreed to be on her team. Initially, he'd suggested that they should be on separate teams, to challenge her boastful comment about being excellent at quizzes. She'd pouted and he'd caved, which was a good thing, because he probably would have been losing otherwise. But he didn't usually give in to people's small manipulations that way.

As well as vast general knowledge, Deepti could discern patterns and make connections faster than even he could. He was fascinated by the way her mind worked.

Although, truth be told, he was finding himself fascinated by everything about her. She was so different from the women he usually dated. She fell firmly into the danger zone of women who wanted, or needed, to be in relationships. And he was definitely not that kind of man.

It was lucky they'd been interrupted in the cinema room before he had managed to kiss her. That would have been a big mistake.

Had she even realised that had been his intention? She hadn't said anything about it on their walk that afternoon, and he had no plans to bring it up. But then, she'd been unusually quiet and a little reflective. There had been something on her mind.

He silently observed her as she laughed and joked with the crew members who'd joined them. With Chef, she was completely at ease. But that made sense; they were long-standing friends and she openly admitted he was the reason she'd got the job as assistant chef.

Whatever had been on her mind earlier that day seemed to have been put behind her now. He wished she had opened up to him about it. She wasn't being completely open with him and, although she was entitled to keep things private, he couldn't help suspect there was something behind her evasiveness.

He tutted his frustration. He was spending too much time thinking about Deepti. He shouldn't be this interested in her. She would be gone from his life soon. The hollowness in his chest showed it would be a good idea to limit their interactions going forward to when Bella was around.

When the pub quiz host announced that their team had won, Deepti stood up and cheered and then threw her arms around him. He stood frozen by the unexpected gesture, causing Deepti to stiffen and draw back quickly. He was about to draw her back to him when Alex came over to hug her. Matteo frowned. He knew they were close but was there something more between them? Not that it was any of his business if there was, but before that evening the only interaction he'd seen between them was as friends, so he had assumed that was all they were.

A bottle of champagne and a gift certificate was brought over to their table. They decided to finish the champagne there rather than take it back to the hotel. At least the other team members agreed with him that Deepti deserved the gift certificate since she'd been the obvious MVP.

'We're going to join the others clubbing. Why don't you come with us?' one of the crew said as she finished her drink.

'Oh, not for me. I'm not a big dancer,' Deepti replied. 'I think I'll head back to the hotel.'

'What about you, Mr Di Corrado?'

'I'll go back to the hotel with Deepti. Thank you all for inviting me,' he said to the crew. It had been years since he'd been clubbing and, though he enjoyed dancing, he didn't imagine it would be fun without Deepti.

He went outside with some of the others who wanted to find a taxi to the club. Deepti had gone to the bathroom, so Matteo kept an eye on the door. She came through the door with Alex, who had one arm around Deepti and the other around the head steward. When Alex leaned over to kiss the steward, Deepti moved out from under his arm, giving the two of them space.

Matteo couldn't explain why he felt such relief at the unspoken clarification that Deepti and Chef weren't a couple.

This was getting ridiculous. Deepti was an attractive woman, nothing more. There was nothing special about her. Perhaps after they returned to their hotel suite he would go to one of the bars to see whether he could find alternative company.

He dismissed that thought almost as quickly as it had arisen. He wasn't after female company generally—that and Deepti weren't interchangeable. He wasn't interested in spending time with anyone else.

'Are you ready to head back now?' Matteo asked Deepti. 'I can call for a car.'

Deepti gave him a sweet, almost sad smile. 'I was thinking I may take a walk along the beachfront. It's well-lit and the hotel's only a thirty-minute walk.' She turned to Alex. Matteo was sure she was about to ask him to accompany her.

'That's fine. I'll walk with you.' As Deepti opened her mouth, he held up his hand. 'I could do with some fresh air too.'

She gave him a brief nod, then turned to say her goodbyes to the rest of the crew. Alex whispered something in her ear, which made her give a shocked laugh and playfully push on his arm.

They walked along the beach road in companionable silence for a few minutes until Deepti said, 'You're quite the quiz maestro. I have to admit, I was surprised.'

'Surprised? Why?'

'I don't know. I never thought it would be your kind of activity. But you've constantly challenged my preconceptions.'

Matteo stood still. 'What preconceptions did you have?' he asked, intrigued.

Deepti came to a halt too, then turned to look up at him. 'I don't know. Taking part in a pub quiz just isn't something I imagined you would spend your free time doing.'

'It has been a while since I've taken part in a pub quiz, but I often enter charity quizzes.' He smiled. 'Growing up, Luca and I were quite the team. We had complementary interests and skills, which helped.'

'Do you always win?' she asked.

'Generally.'

She beamed at him. 'Of course you always win. I don't know why I asked. Are you both quite competitive, then?' She must have realised she'd referred to his brother in the present tense because her smile faltered and she bit her lip.

'Yes, we both liked to win. But we weren't usually in competition with each other.'

*Apart from over women, apparently.* Matteo paused. Before that caustic thought had crossed his mind, it had been the first time he'd spoken and reminisced about Luca without the sting of betrayal and anger. He swallowed. It had also been a long time since he'd used his brother's name—referring to him as 'my brother' made it easier to maintain the distance in his thoughts too. But Luca's name had slipped out so easily while he'd been talking to Deepti.

For the first time since Luca had passed away, all he felt was an overwhelming sense of loss.

She crooked her head, waiting for him to speak. When he didn't, she gave him a small, shy smile before leaving the path and walking on to the sand, towards the water. She stood peacefully, looking out at the darkness.

He studied Deepti's profile in the moonlight.

What was it about her that put him at ease? She was so breathtakingly beautiful. Not supermodel, magazine-cover beautiful but, in his opinion, every single facial feature was perfect.

His eyes rested on the contours of her full lips. What would she do if he cupped her chin to turn her mouth up to his? Would she move away or would she rise to meet his lips?

He swallowed and moved his gaze towards the road, watching the lights of the cars pass.

'Matteo, is everything all right?' Deepti put her hand on his arm.

'It's fine. We should go.'

He shook off her hand and hurried forward. In his haste as he moved away, he tripped over his feet. He could have stopped himself from falling if he hadn't sensed Deepti's hands reach out to grab him. Trying to avoid her touch, he continued to fall. His weight and momentum were too strong for her restraining efforts and she toppled over with him.

He managed to land on his back, so she fell directly on top of him rather than onto the ground. His heart was racing. He groaned as his body reacted immediately to her movements when she continued to wriggle against him in an effort to get up.

'Could you stop that please?' he said stiffly. She stilled immediately. 'Sorry.'

'It's okay.' He desperately wanted to put his arms round her and gather her even closer to his chest. He wanted to turn her onto her back and kiss her until she moaned for him.

Instead, he closed his eyes to gather his peace. Then he helped Deepti sit up, the new position doing nothing to help his equilibrium, but, once upright, Deepti was able to climb off him.

She held out a hand to help pull him up.

'Probably not a good idea,' he said, refusing her offer. 'I'll only make you fall over again.'

Deepti cleared her throat and walked a few steps away.

Matteo stood up and brushed the sand off his clothes. He couldn't believe he'd tripped. He had a great sense of balance. It was because of Deepti. She constantly had him off-kilter and confused.

He wanted her. He wanted to sleep with her. That was out of the question while she was Bella's companion. Even their almost-kiss in the cinema room had been wrong.

But when they arrived in Singapore she wouldn't be under his charge any more. He could ask her whether she wanted to get together with him before she left for England.

But he had to be clear exactly what he was offering her. He would love to spend more time with her, and he very much wanted to make love to her. But there would be no question of a relationship. It would be a brief affair, a fling at most. She'd already told him she was planning to return to England soon after they got to Singapore. He couldn't see a reason to ask her to change her plans.

As long as she knew he would never have romantic feelings for her, for anyone ever again, then they could have a few days of string-free fun together.

As he watched her walk ahead and away from him in the moonlight, an unexpected heaviness filled his chest and he couldn't help feeling it was the prospect of saying goodbye.

## CHAPTER ELEVEN

IT WAS HARD to believe they'd already been at sea for over a month and there were now only a few days left until they reached Singapore. Life on a luxurious super-yacht was the definition of smooth sailing.

As Deepti was heading to Matteo's lounge to give him an update on Bella, Jack met her in the foyer to let her know Matteo was waiting out on his deck.

While they'd been at sea over the past week, Matteo had been busy with business meetings, and had had guests on board, so it would be the first time she'd seen him since they'd left Abu Dhabi. Although, Matteo had been a prominent feature in Deepti's dreams since that day.

She kept replaying the fall on the beach. If it had happened like in one of her beloved Asian dramas, when Matteo had fallen, taking her with him, she would have accidentally landed with her mouth on his. She laughed at the image—if only reality could be as simple as that.

He wasn't smiling when she walked out onto the deck. Deepti looked down, unable to meet his gaze, wondering if he ever thought about that night.

'Is this a good time?' she asked, for something to break the silence.

He nodded, still unsmiling. 'Tomorrow we're going to reach Malaysia. The *Serendipity* is going to anchor off a private island owned by my friend. This will be our last catch-up of the trip.'

She frowned. The catch-ups hadn't been necessary for a while. Why had he chosen that day to stop them?

'I asked Chef to send up some food,' he said, gesturing towards a table which had a charcuterie board, platters of fruit and cheese and a tiered stand with macaroons and *petits fours*. 'I hope it's okay to offer the desserts you made.' His smile brightened his face and lightened the atmosphere. 'Take a seat while I pour the drinks.'

She quickly gave Matteo a rundown of what she and Bella had been doing for the past week.

'She seems to have coped well with the sailing, but I think she's ready to be on land now,' Deepti said to end her update.

'And what about you? How did you cope with sailing?'

'It's been fine. I mean, this yacht moves so smoothly, it's hard to believe we're on water, even when it's at anchor. Has it been a success-ful trip for you?'

Either he hadn't heard her question or he ignored it.

'This was your first sail, wasn't it?' he asked.

'It was.'

'Did you enjoy it? Do you think you'd sign on to crew again?'

Deepti didn't know how to answer. She loved sailing but she'd joined the crew to escape from the past for a few weeks, not to make it a career path. 'Never say never.'

'So what is your plan when you return to London? You said you wanted to find a new job, but you didn't say what. I assumed you would work as a pastry chef, but is that the case?'

Deepti shrugged. She didn't want to lie to Matteo but she didn't want to spoil her last few days by bringing up the past. How could she trust that Matteo wouldn't judge her the way her colleagues had—people who had known her for years—when she had only known him a few weeks?

And it would be difficult to explain the situation without bringing up her ex-boyfriend. Even if, by a slim chance, Matteo believed she hadn't been at fault for losing the client and deal, he might still judge her as having been unwise to trust her ex-boyfriend. The past few weeks—getting to spend time with someone who had no knowledge of her previous career, her ex-boyfriend or the troubles he'd brought on her—had been a joy. What benefit would there be in telling the truth now?

'How long are you planning to stay in Singapore?' he asked.

Deepti tilted her head. Something was going on with Matteo—there was an intensity and a quiet pent-up emotion. She didn't know what could be causing it. And she didn't know whether it was her place to ask. It was a strange position to be in—not exactly his employee or colleague but also not quite a friend, and definitely not a lover.

She decided to take his question at face value. 'I haven't booked my return ticket yet. Alex suggested I wait in case there were any delays along the voyage. But I have a long list of places I want to visit, so I'll probably stay a few days. How about you? Are you working while you're there or will you spend time with your parents?'

'Working. My parents and I… We're not close.' His whole body had become rigid and his shoulders were tight.

'You seem tense,' Deepti said. 'Has it been a while since you've seen your parents?'

Matteo pressed his lips together and the muscle in his jaw tightened. Deepti cursed inwardly that she'd ruined the mood by asking the question directly.

'Six years,' he replied curtly.

'Oh, that's how long you said it had been since you saw your brother,' she said, then froze. There had clearly been an issue between Matteo and his brother, and now it sounded as if it had repercussions for his parents as well.

Matteo inhaled sharply. 'Yes, we stopped talking at the same time. They took my brother's side.'

'I see. That must have hurt.' She stared at him without blinking. If he didn't want to say anything else, if he didn't want to give any explanations, that would be fine. She wasn't going to pry or ask any questions.

'It did,' he said. 'This wasn't a situation with ambiguity. My brother had an affair with my fiancée. I found out when they told me she was pregnant. My parents agreed what they did was wrong, but they refused to break off contact with them, even though the alternative was to lose me.' He clamped his lips together and looked away from her.

Deepti blinked. She shook her head then blinked again. Had she heard him correctly—Matteo's fiancée had cheated on him with his brother? And his parents had sided with his brother. She didn't understand how they could do that.

She wanted to wrap him in her arms and protect him from the world and anybody who'd ever hurt him. Instead, she reached for his hand and held it between her own. 'I am so sorry that happened to you.'

'It was a long time ago.' He sounded as if he was brushing off her concern but he put his free hand over their clasped ones.

'I don't think there's a time limit on how much that must have hurt you.'

'With hindsight, I know Lauren—my ex-fiancée—wasn't the right person for me. I should have realised I'm not the marrying kind. Work will always be my priority. And, before you ask, there was no need for a paternity test; there's no chance Bella's mine.'

The thought hadn't crossed her mind. But now she was curious.

As if to answer her unspoken question, Matteo said, 'I was so busy building up the business, I barely had any time to spend with Lauren. There was no way I could have got her pregnant. That should have been a sign that everything wasn't right but I ignored it.

'She was exactly the kind of woman I thought would make the perfect CEO's wife. We'd been together for a couple of years and asking her to marry me seemed like the next logical step. At that young age, I thought marriage and children were the boxes I needed to tick to be successful in life.' He gave a bitter laugh. 'I know better now. I'm never going down that road again.'

When Matteo mentioned not being the marrying kind, it caused an ache in Deepti's chest. She could understand the betrayal could make him wary. What her ex had done had made her feel as if she couldn't trust anyone again and it was nothing compared to what Matteo had experienced. But Matteo deserved to be loved and to find someone who loved him deeply in return.

She shook her head. This wasn't about Matteo's future relationships and what she wanted for him. It was about his past.

'You were very close as brothers before, weren't you?' she said. 'I can't imagine what that was like for you, to find out.' And for him to treat Bella as an innocent child, and not the living reminder of having been cheated on, made her admire him even more.

'I was close to Luca. He was my best friend as well as family. We did nearly everything together. I wanted him to join my business and work with me to get it off the ground. Instead, he went after my fiancée. It was a huge betrayal.

And I ignored all their attempts at justifying what they did. The sad thing is, I always thought one day we'd reconcile. That our brotherly bond would be stronger than what happened and all it would take was a bit of distance, particularly when I realised Lauren wasn't right for me. But I left it too late. I never thought we'd run out of time.'

Without saying a word, Deepti opened out her arms. Matteo expelled a sharp breath and walked into the comfort she offered.

He held on tightly; she didn't even attempt to let go until he was ready.

When they finally did pull apart, still holding each other but with space between their bodies, there was the sheen of moisture around his eyes. She reached out, but at the last second she avoided wiping his tears and touched his hair, moving his fringe to the side unnecessarily, leaving her hand cupping the side of his face.

They gazed into each other's eyes without saying a word. Almost in slow motion, Matteo leaned forward and planted a quick kiss on her lips so fast, it was over in the blink of an eye, and yet Deepti's whole body fired into life at that brief connection.

She swallowed. Matteo was holding his breath, waging an inner battle with himself. She'd wanted this for so long. Perhaps it wasn't the best time, coming after such an emotional revelation, but she had to seize the chance.

In a moment of perfect synchronicity, they moved closer, their mouths seeking and finding each other's, clinging and devouring, the touch of their tongues sending spirals of desire right through her.

Without warning he broke off and pushed her gently away, his breath fast and heavy. He walked away without a word.

# CHAPTER TWELVE

DEEPTI COULDN'T IMAGINE a more idyllic setting as she helped Bella build a sandcastle on the pristine, white sandy beach of a private island near Malaysia. They were spending their last couple of days here before arriving in Singapore. If only her mind could be a quarter as peaceful as the gentle ocean waves lapping against the shore.

Since they hadn't been able to dock near the island, they'd had to anchor *Serendipity* some distance away. To get to the island, she, Tracey and the children had been dropped off by the yacht's speedboat straight after breakfast.

They'd been playing for a couple of hours, and now the children were getting hungry, so Tracey suggested they head back to the yacht. Deepti was about to page the yacht to get one of the watercrafts out to collect them when Tracey put a restraining hand on her arm.

'Just wait,' Tracey said. 'It looks like someone is coming.'

Deepti followed the direction of Tracey's gaze. Her throat went dry as she recognised the imposing outline of Matteo silhouetted against the horizon. He was followed by two people carrying picnic baskets.

'Hi,' Matteo said, as he approached them. 'I thought it would be nice if we all had lunch together. Chef has prepared something amazing for us.'

Bella ran over and threw herself into his arms. He pressed a quick kiss on the top of her head. Holding hands, Matteo and Bella helped lay out the picnic blanket and take the dishes out of the basket.

While they ate, Deepti casually tried to glance at him. She didn't want to get caught staring, but she was downfallen to find out he'd never looked in her direction anyway.

Had he thought about last night at all or had he managed to put it behind him already? He had seemed as into their kiss as she was but then he'd all but pushed her away. She'd stayed where she was on the deck for ten minutes after he'd gone, hoping…wishing…he'd come back.

She sighed. Why was she sad? Matteo had been right to stop things when he had.

He had barely said two words to her since he'd arrived on the island. Was he purposely keeping his distance? Was he worried that she would read more into the kiss than the culmination of a mutual attraction? She knew it wasn't going anywhere. They would reach Singapore the next day and she would return to England soon afterwards. What was the point of giving in to the attraction when there was no way to act on it?

If only their kiss hadn't been so perfect, hadn't made her long for more. Hadn't started her wondering what might have been.

After they'd finished eating, Bella grabbed Matteo's hand and took him to the dunes they'd discovered earlier. Deepti's heart twisted when she heard Bella's easy laughter. He was such a kind and loving uncle. She could now understand his initial distance towards Bella and Leo—their parents had betrayed him in the worst possible way. Looking at the way he was interacting with them now, and how comfortably Bella leaned against Matteo while she showed him her discovery, she could see no resentment at all towards the innocent children. The only emotion evident was deep affection, even love.

At least he was able to open his heart to some people. She hoped it meant he would be willing to listen to his parents in time. Although she understood how he felt and was completely on his side, he'd spoken about having run out of time with his brother—she hoped he would feel differently about resolving things with his parents.

And maybe one day he would be ready to open his heart to a woman again. He deserved to be loved by someone wholeheartedly and without reservation. Deepti rubbed her chest as she felt a pang, knowing she couldn't be that woman. Why did she have these feelings about Matteo? What was it about him that made her long for things which were impossible?

Were her feelings about Matteo caught up in the general confusion that her life had been in over the past few months? She'd thought she was in a stable job with good career prospects. She had thought she was in a stable relationship. Neither of those had been true. She seemed to be making one mistake after another. How she could she trust what she was thinking, what she was feeling, now?

Matteo had been betrayed by people he'd loved. It didn't take a psychologist to see that experience had made him wary and mistrustful. How could she ask him to trust her when she hadn't been open with him?

Her reasons for not telling him about being fired from her job had always been weak. She'd initially convinced herself she didn't want him to know because he was her employer and she didn't want to risk getting fired from another job. The truth was her reasons were based in protecting herself from the humiliation of what had happened. People who'd worked closely with her for years had been so ready to believe the worst in her. Why should she expect Matteo to believe in her when he'd known her a far shorter time? She couldn't expect the same unquestioning loyalty from him as she had from her parents or Alex.

And why did it matter if he didn't believe her? But it did matter…a lot.

'Me and the kids should head back. I'll put them down for their naps,' Tracey said as she cleared away the lunch plates. Deepti started gathering things too.

'You don't have to come, Dee,' Tracey said. 'Didn't you say you wanted to explore the island? I'm sure it's safe for you.'

'I can stay with you, Deepti. I've been here a couple of times. I don't mind showing you around,' Matteo said.

That didn't sound like the most sensible idea. With her thoughts in such turmoil, not to mention her jumbled feelings, she knew that it was safest for her heart if she wasn't in his company as much.

'Oh, that's okay, thank you,' she said. 'I may as well return with you all.'

'That would be a shame, Dee,' Tracey said.

'The kids will be sleeping so there's nothing for you to do on board. And why waste the opportunity of being on this beautiful island rather than being cooped up on the yacht?'

Again a variety of emotions warred for supremacy. Ultimately, she only had a limited amount of time to spend with Matteo. She could control her feelings and simply enjoy his company.

'Okay, I guess I will stay, since you're planning to come back after the children's naps.' She turned to Matteo, shielding her eyes from the sun as she lifted her head. 'You don't have to stay. I'm sure you've got a lot of business to deal with.'

Matteo grinned. 'No. I made such great progress, I've decided to take the afternoon off.'

Deepti blinked. 'A day off? Are you sure the markets will survive?'

Matteo grinned. 'There's only one way to find out.'

They all went to the island jetty. Next to the waiting speedboat was a jet ski on which Matteo had come over from the yacht, while the crew had brought the picnic in the speedboat.

'Do you have your swimming costume on?' Matteo asked after the speedboat left.

Deepti nodded.

'There's a place I'd like to show you, but it

will be faster if we go round the island on the jet ski rather than go on land.'

Deepti eyed the single jet ski. She hadn't been on one before so part of her was glad she wouldn't have to control the machine herself. On the other hand, sitting behind Matteo with him between her knees and her arms around his waist, her greater concern was whether she would be able to control her own reactions.

They took the jet ski to the other side, which had a small beach which led quickly into lush vegetation.

'It's through this forest,' Matteo said. 'It can be a little dark once we're in, but I promise the journey will be worth it.'

She could sense his supressed excitement about their destination. 'Lead the way, then,' she said, repeating the arm gesture she'd made when they'd been about to take the hidden path in Fiore. She wasn't sure if he remembered but he reached for her hand.

'To be safe,' he said.

After walking for about ten minutes, Deepti could hear thundering. She couldn't quite define the sound, but it was calming rather than frightening.

'Almost there,' Matteo said, tugging her hand slightly to make her walk faster.

The thundering got louder and she could

smell fresh water. When they reached a clearing, Deepti inhaled sharply as she took in a mesmerising cascade of crystal-clear water flowing down a straight drop into a turquoise pool.

Matteo had seen the waterfall before. But seeing the different expressions chase across Deepti's face made him look at it again, as if seeing it for the first time.

When he'd first decided to take her there, he had imagined various ways she would react to the site, but Deepti throwing her head back and laughing deeply and uninhibitedly was a delicious surprise.

His lips twitched, even though he felt as if he'd missed the joke. Then as she carried on giggling without saying anything he understood she was experiencing pure joy. His smile grew wider and he gave in to his impulse to pick her up and twirl her around. She threw her arms around his neck.

'Is this the first time you've seen a waterfall?' he asked.

'Actually, no. I've been to the Niagara Falls. That was impressive, but this actually took my breath away. Is it natural? Something this perfect can't be man-made but I can't understand how there can be a waterfall practically in the middle of an island when there doesn't appear to be an obvious area of elevation or any rivers inland.'

Again, her mind completely captivated him. 'What is going in that beautiful head of yours?'

His question seemed to fluster her. Or was it his compliment?

'The topography of the island is fascinating.'

'The topography? If you think that's interesting, do you want to go for a dip?' Matteo suggested.

'Sure?' Her expression was dubious but he knew she wouldn't turn down the chance to swim in the plunge pool.

He tried not to watch as Deepti threw off her top and shorts. But he failed and his eyes followed her lithe figure as she ran to the edge of the pool.

He expected her to move close to the shallowest area, to where the water met the land, and dip her toe in to test the temperature but, of course, she didn't do the expected.

She looked over at him, calling out, 'Aren't you coming in?' before she took a running leap into the water.

He waited for her to resurface, which she did with a whoop.

'How is it warm?' she asked, laughing as she scooped water in her hands before letting it run through her fingers. Her reaction was exactly what he'd been waiting for. Despite the beautiful scenery around him, it was her glorious smile that captivated him. His eyes homed in on her mouth, on those lush lips that tasted so sweet. He shook his head to clear the memory.

'No idea,' he said. 'I could ask my friend, if you really want to know.'

'I kind of do. As long as it's not artificially heated. If it is, then let me remain in ignorant bliss.' She giggled. 'Aren't you coming in?'

He wasn't sure that was the wisest move to take but he couldn't resist the chance to be in the water with her. He removed his shirt and shorts and folded them neatly, putting them in a pile on a rock. Then he picked up Deepti's discarded clothes and did the same.

When he turned back to the pool, Deepti hastily lifted her gaze. He smirked at almost catching her staring at his backside.

Following Deepti's lead, he jumped into the pool, purposely trying to make the biggest splash he could. He surfaced to Deepti's wide-eyed, disbelieving face.

'I can't believe you did that!' she exclaimed, and he knew he could expect retaliation.

They played in the water like a couple of school children—carefree and relaxed. He had meant to keep a physical distance between them at all times but his body wasn't paying any attention to his brain.

Following his lead, they swam closer to the cascade, basking in the spray. Wading over to where she was treading water, he took her into his arms. Deepti clearly guessed where he was heading and tightened her arms around his neck. When she wrapped her legs around his waist, his body jerked to life. He gulped and forced his feet to move forward, knowing that being plunged under the cold, rushing water was exactly what he needed at that moment.

Matteo put Deepti down on the ledge behind the drop. He watched her as she soaked in the view.

With wet hair plastered to her head, and not a trace of make-up, she was still stunning. Her sheer, open joy and wonderment at what she was seeing animated her face. He desperately wanted to kiss her again.

They still hadn't spoken about the previous evening. He was still processing why he'd opened up to her in the first place. The only people who knew about the past were his family—the people directly involved in it. He'd never shared the truth with anybody. Why Deepti?

He'd had brief, pretty meaningless relationships over the years. A physical relationship was nothing unusual. Kissing Deepti didn't have to have a special meaning but it had felt different.

It was too loud to talk near the waterfall. They had been in the water longer than he'd planned, but for a brief moment he wished their idyllic time didn't have to end.

They should start making their way back to the beach. They stood there for a few minutes more before Matteo held out his hand to help Deepti back under the cascade and into the pool. Deepti swam over to the side near their clothes but, instead of climbing out of the water, she leaned back against the bank.

He waded over to her.

'We probably should get out and get back to the yacht,' he said.

She nodded but didn't say anything. She just stared at him. He moved closer, until their bodies were almost touching. He waited, giving her the chance to move away if she wanted to.

She didn't. She licked her lips and swallowed.

He put his hands on the bank on either side of her shoulders and waited again. When she remained still, he stepped forward again until their bodies were finally in contact, the heat emanating from the contact rivalling the source of the thermal waters.

Slowly, he bent his head closer. She lifted her mouth to meet his questing lips. They kissed hungrily until he tried to break away. This time, Deepti didn't let him go. She made a murmur of protest then moved up against him and held his head down to hers. He hoisted her up and she wrapped her legs around him as he carried her onto the bank and laid her down.

Their kisses became deeper and more passionate, and rational thought only prevailed when he felt her hand on the waistband of his swimming trunks. If he didn't put a halt to things right then, it would lead to the inevitable conclusion. And he didn't want to make love to her in the open, regardless of how romantic the setting was.

He pulled away and sat up, breathing deeply, trying to get the air back into his lungs. He laughed at Deepti's instinctive grunt of protest. She reached out for him again. He pressed a quick kiss to her lips.

'We have to stop,' he said.

'Why?'

He didn't know why the single word, a mix of question and protest, made his chest tighten but the urge to throw caution to the wind was strong. He turned away so he couldn't be tempted. 'I don't have any protection with me, for one thing.'

He heard her gasp and sensed her sit up. 'I don't have any with me either.'

She reached over for her clothes and handed

his to him. 'You're right. We should get back to the yacht.'

He didn't want this to be the end of their physical relationship. He liked spending time with Deepti but he had never tried to deny he was very attracted to her. Back in England, he would have invited her out for dinner. He would have set the boundaries then, making it clear that the most he could offer her was a short affair, a fling. He was too broken and bruised to offer her anything more. Would that be enough for her?

Deepti was too open and kind. He would inevitably hurt her. And, to his surprise, he actually cared about hurting her. He hadn't cared about anyone for a long time.

'We need to talk,' he said.

Although Deepti knew Matteo was right, and they needed to talk, she wished it wasn't necessary.

They left the waterfall and walked back to the jet ski. She sat behind him and wrapped her arms around his waist. It felt like the end of something beautiful. As they moved off, she rested her head against his back and willed herself not to become emotional.

When they got to the beach, they sat on the blanket left there from that morning. Matteo's expression was a grim mixture of anger and regret.

Deepti's first inclination was to brush off their embrace, to tell Matteo it didn't matter. She wanted to protect herself from further pain. But that would be a lie—it did matter. And, just as it had hurt her when he'd pushed her away after they'd kissed for the first time, it hurt her again now that he'd stopped things from going much further—even though the rational part of her brain knew it was the wisest decision when they didn't have any way of having safe sex. But was that the only reason he'd stopped? She couldn't help feeling there was more to it.

She sighed. Why couldn't things be simple? If they'd met anywhere else, they could have acted on their attraction without worrying about the circumstances.

Deepti scoffed. They moved in completely different worlds. The chances of them having met anywhere else was miniscule. Even on the yacht, there wouldn't usually be much interaction between the owner and her as assistant chef.

If Bella hadn't found her that first day and somehow become attached to her, then she wouldn't be on this island half-naked next to Matteo minutes after the most passionate embrace of her life.

She realised her mind had wandered when Matteo cleared his throat and then said, 'About what just happened—it was a mistake. I shouldn't have done that.'

Why did hearing that feel like a knife to her heart?

'I understand,' she said, looking anywhere but at him. He was right: they shouldn't have kissed. She was Bella's companion, and it was inappropriate for her to kiss Matteo. If only she'd brought a cardigan with her, or something more substantial than a coverall; she suddenly felt chilled and needed to get away. She stood up, trying to gather the last remaining items they'd brought out.

'Can you sit down please?' Matteo asked. 'I'd like us to talk here, in privacy.'

Deepti's eyes widened. There was more to say? She sat down again but kept a safe distance from Matteo's magnetic warmth.

'It's important to be open and up front from the start so there are no misunderstandings,' Matteo said.

'Absolutely,' Deepti agreed, while reflecting she'd never had such a conversation in the past. She couldn't imagine him wanting such a conversation up front was going to herald anything good. Usually, she started dating without any discussions about expectations.

'You're a beautiful woman. I can't deny I am very attracted to you.'

Deepti's spirits rose at his simple statement… then came crashing back down. 'But…?' she prompted, knowing one was coming.

'But, while we're on the yacht, it's not appropriate for us to have an affair.'

She wanted to protest that they literally weren't on the yacht, but she knew that wasn't what he was talking about. Then she paused and tilted her head. Was he implying that things could be different once they reached Singapore, or was she reading far too much into a simple, declarative statement?

'We're only on the yacht for another night,' she pointed out.

Matteo grinned. Her heart needed to get used to him doing that—its constant flipping couldn't be good for her. 'That's right. And, once we've dropped Bella and Leo off with my parents, you won't be working as her companion anymore.'

'And would things be more appropriate then?' She spoke slowly. She didn't want to invite rejection but she wanted to be crystal-clear she knew where she stood.

Again, that devastating grin with his adorable dimples appeared. 'I think they would be.'

Deepti lost the ability to talk. She couldn't even remember how to breathe. Matteo was agreeing to a relationship with her once they arrived in Singapore.

'I want to be clear what I'm offering,' Matteo said. 'I don't do relationships.'

Deepti's heart dipped, but she could understand why Matteo wasn't keen on relationships after his experience with his fiancée.

'So what are you offering?' she asked.

'A brief affair or fling while you're in Singapore. You said you were flying back in a few days. Why don't we spend time together until then?'

'And after that it will be over,' Deepti said. It was a statement, not a question; she wanted to make sure everything was spelled out.

'That's right. I don't want to lead you on, making you believe this is the start of something long-term, or love and marriage are in the future, because that's just not possible.'

Deepti was silent, digesting what he was saying. Really, it was what she'd been expecting, but the little hope which had been alive in her that this was the beginning of something real, not the end, shrivelled completely at the stark reality.

She liked Matteo. He was the most attractive man she'd ever met. She enjoyed spending time with him. Every nerve in her body was urging her to agree to his terms and spend a few blissful days in his arms and in his bed. But a quieter, more rational part of her knew she would be in danger of falling even more deeply for him if she agreed to their fling.

It would be safer for her heart if they left things the way they were. The only question was, did she want to be safe?

# CHAPTER THIRTEEN

DEEPTI STOOD ON deck with Alex and other members of the crew as *Serendipity* sailed into Keppel Bay.

They'd finally reached Singapore.

Conflicting emotions warred within Deepti: excitement at the prospect of finally exploring a country she'd dreamed of visiting for years; dread at the idea she would soon have to return to England and face her future; sadness at having to say goodbye to Bella and Leo; complete confusion at the situation with Matteo.

She'd tried to keep herself busy since they'd left the private island and returned to the yacht. Any moment she hadn't been occupied, she'd been thinking about Matteo's proposition.

Why was this a difficult decision? She liked Matteo and she was incredibly attracted to him. She definitely wanted to sleep with him. What was preventing her from saying yes?

He'd made it clear that a short fling was all

he would offer, which was perfect for her, since that was all she could deal with until she managed to get the rest of her life sorted out.

And, after he had been so open and honest with her about his fiancée and his brother, she understood why he didn't believe in long-term relationships. He'd been betrayed. There was no other way of putting it. She couldn't imagine going through what he had. She'd found it hard to trust anything after what had happened to her, and it was nothing in comparison to what had happened to him.

After the betrayal he had experienced at the hands of two people he had loved unconditionally, of course he wasn't ready to give his heart to someone new.

She hoped one day he would be ready. She'd seen how he'd spent time with Bella and Leo, even though Bella was the physical representation of that betrayal. He had a limitless capacity to love and he deserved to find someone worthy of loving him in return.

And that wasn't her. Though she would never, could never, cheat on someone, she wasn't going to tell Matteo the whole truth behind why she was on *Serendipity*. She was still lying to him, hiding a core part of herself. She was in many ways no better than the people he'd trusted before who'd let him down.

In a few hours, unless she agreed to his suggestion that they have a brief affair before she returned to England, she might be saying goodbye to Matteo for good and she would never see him again.

She rubbed her chest, as if trying to ease the heaviness inside her at the prospect of never seeing Matteo again.

If she did want to agree to having a fling with Matteo, telling him the truth at this late stage could ruin things. She enjoyed being with him without the weight of her past and the fallout of her ex-boyfriend's actions affecting their time together. If a long-term relationship had been a possibility, then maybe she would have told Matteo the truth, but he had made it clear they could only have a fling. He'd told her he wasn't the marrying kind so there was no real reason to tell him what had happened.

Bella calling her name, excited that the yacht had docked, brought her back to reality.

As they disembarked, she came face to face with Matteo. He briefly inclined his head but there was no outward indication that anything had happened between them on the island. But what did she expect? They were surrounded by people. He couldn't very well bring up their kiss in front of everybody.

A car was waiting for them and soon they

were crossing Keppel Bridge towards the main part of Singapore, heading towards Matteo's parents' house. Even though he was seated in front of her, something in his posture suggested he was feeling tense.

As she got out of the car when they arrived, she walked up to Matteo and briefly pressed his hand, before moving to Bella to help her get ready to meet her grandparents.

A maid opened the door to them and a distinguished-looking older couple came out to the foyer while Deepti was helping Bella take off her jacket. She would have known these were Matteo's parents anywhere. He'd inherited his father's height and strong jawline, and his mother's cheekbones and wavy hair.

'Matteo,' the woman said, holding out her arms to him.

'Mother,' Matteo replied, remaining where he was.

Deepti watched the sadness cross the woman's face as she put down her arms. She could understand why Matteo wasn't rushing to embrace his parents, but she could also imagine how his mother felt, losing one son and being estranged from her only remaining child.

'Bella, do you remember your grandparents?' Deepti asked, bringing Bella forward, since the little girl had hidden behind her. 'I think you last saw them when Leo was born. Say hello, sweetie.'

Bella shook her head and hid her face on Deepti's leg.

'Why don't we go through to the drawing room?' Matteo's father suggested. 'We can get something to eat and drink.'

Bella snuggled further into Deepti's side.

'That would be very nice,' Deepti responded with a welcome smile as they all followed the parents.

'Let me introduce you,' Matteo said, once they were seated. 'Deepti, these are my parents. Mother, Father, this is Deepti Roy, Bella's companion. I sent you a message about her.'

'Yes, of course,' Matteo's mum said. 'Thank you for stepping in to help out with our Bella. It was reassuring to hear she was okay for the journey.'

'Excuse me for interrupting,' Tracey said. 'Is there anywhere I can change Leo? And he should probably take a nap soon.'

'Of course,' Matteo's mother said. 'Why don't I show you his nursery? And I can show you your room as well. Bella, do you want to come with me?' She put out her hand.

Bella crawled onto Deepti's lap and began to suck her thumb. Deepti threw a worried glance at Matteo—Bella had never done that before.

'I want to see your room, Bella,' Deepti said. 'Why don't we go with Tracey and Leo?' She realised immediately that Matteo would be left alone with his father. She didn't want Matteo to be uncomfortable, but she didn't want to overstep the boundaries of whatever was between them.

She hadn't anticipated Bella's behaviour regressing. Perhaps she should have given more thought to what could go wrong with the handover.

All she'd thought about was Matteo's proposition. Even now she was thinking about giving him her answer. Was that the person she'd become? But what choice did she have? She couldn't stay with Bella for ever.

She left Tracey trying to put Bella down for a nap and went back to the drawing room. Matteo was standing near a cabinet while his parents were seated. His body was facing away from them. She almost shivered from the coolness in the atmosphere in the room.

'Ah, Deepti, come in. Sit down, please,' Matteo's father said as she walked in. 'We've been discussing this situation with Bella. And I would like to ask you to stay on for a few days to help Bella with the transition. Tracey said Bella opened up to her after you'd been interacting for a few days. Hopefully, Bella will open to her grandma and me.'

'Please do agree,' Matteo's mother said. 'We can have a guest room prepared for you. And you would have your evenings free. It would be the same arrangement you had on the yacht.'

Deepti cast a glance at Matteo but his expression was inscrutable. She took a deep breath. Now she had two offers to consider—this was no time for her to be indecisive.

This time, the answer came easily to her.

'Thank you for the offer,' Deepti said. 'And I'm very happy to help Bella with a transition, but it can only be for a few days.'

Another glance at Matte showed his jaw clench and he walked to the window, turning his back on the room.

'I'm very happy to stay here overnight,' Deepti continued. 'But after tonight I don't think it's a good idea for me to be in the same house. The whole point is for Bella to get used to me not being around.' She took a deep breath to steel her nerves. 'Matteo, perhaps you could help me organise a hotel room? Maybe where you're staying?'

Matteo turned back to her, his eyebrows raised in a question.

She smiled shyly at him. It was really difficult to convey her answer to his proposition when she was the centre of attention of his parents. It went without saying that he wouldn't want his parents to know about their fling.

'I'm sure I'll be able to sort out a room for you,' he told her, flashing a bright grin. 'I should head off now. I'll let you know if there are any problems. Why don't I contact you later this evening? We can sort when and where we'll meet tomorrow.'

Deepti nodded, biting her lip to contain the happiness bubbling inside her at the prospect of her fling with Matteo.

'Matteo, aren't you going to stay for lunch?' his mother asked, sounding slightly upset.

'I'm afraid I have a meeting soon and I need to get to the office first.'

'Uncle Mayo, will you read my story tonight?' Bella asked, coming into the room, followed by an apologetic Tracey.

Deepti could tell Matteo was torn. He didn't want to disappoint his niece but the tension between his parents and him was palpable.

'Can't I read your story tonight, sweetie?' Deepti asked Bella.

Bella pouted. She'd got used to her uncle being part of her bedtime routine. It was probably going to be just as difficult to transition Bella off Matteo.

'Why don't you come for dinner, Matteo? Then you can read to Bella.'

Matteo visibly stiffened at his mother's suggestion. Deepti's heart went out to him. She understood the betrayal he must have felt when his parents had supported his brother. But Matteo had admitted himself that he'd always thought he would reconcile with Luca, who it was clear he'd loved very much.

'I'm afraid I have a dinner meeting, mother,' Matteo answered.

Deepti was torn. She supported Matteo and how he felt unquestioningly, but at the same time Bella was a five-year-old child and shouldn't be caught in the crossfire of Matteo's fraught relationship with his parents.

'Tracey, I think Bella would like a snack,' Deepti said, wanting to get the little girl out of the room for the rest of the conversation.

'Good idea,' Tracey replied and then excused herself.

Once Bella was out of earshot, Deepti turned to Matteo to ask when he could spare some time for a video call.

'Video call? Matteo, surely you can make time for dinner?' Matteo's father said, putting a comforting hand on his wife's shoulder.

'It's impossible, I'm afraid.' He stared directly at his father.

'Your mother will be disappointed. She was planning to make your favourite dishes.'

Matteo didn't respond. Deepti started shifting weight from one leg to the other in an effort to ignore the uncomfortable silence that had developed. She cleared her throat. 'Is that a no for the video call?'

For a moment, Deepti thought Matteo wasn't going to answer her. Then he gave her a tight smile and nodded. Looking at his cold, aloof expression as he stared at his parents, she missed the carefree, smiling man she'd got to know and like.

Had she made a mistake agreeing to having a fling with Matteo while they were in Singapore? Not because she didn't want to make love with him but Matteo had a lot to deal with without trying to navigate a temporary sexual relationship. And she didn't want to be simply a distraction from his frustrations.

Hopefully, tomorrow they would get the chance to spend some time alone and would be able to talk freely.

But, right at that moment, tomorrow felt a million hours away.

# CHAPTER FOURTEEN

NOT AN IMPATIENT man by nature, Matteo stood at the entrance to Hort Park, waiting for Deepti and the children to arrive.It was typical of Deepti's empathy for her to suggest they meet in a public place rather than his parents' house. He knew it wasn't the proximity to his office that had been behind the suggestion.

He thought about how he'd felt the previous day, seeing his parents for the first time in years. He'd expected their meeting to be stressful. And it had been. He was the one who'd cut them off completely once they'd chosen to keep in contact with Luca—at the time, it had been one betrayal heaped on another, and the last straw for him.

They'd reached out to him on a number of occasions over the years but he'd rebuffed their advances. His parents were understandably wary of where they stood. He should probably let them know this time he was ready and willing to talk. It wasn't going to be an overnight reconciliation, but he was more open to hearing their perspective, although he might never understand it.

But for now he wanted to put the past, and the difficult conversations that were ahead, out of his mind and enjoy his day with the children and his evening with Deepti.

Matteo turned when he heard Bella calling out his name and saw her running towards him. Matteo was surprised to see Tracey with them. Deepti hadn't given any indication that she would be joining them. But, when he heard the reason Tracey had offered to join them was so Deepti could leave with Matteo rather than drop the children back, he was undeniably grateful to her. Again. He had to admit, he'd had several occasions to be grateful to Tracey over the past few weeks for giving him opportunities to spend time alone with Deepti.

His lips quirked. Had his parents unwittingly hired a matchmaker to be their nanny? He didn't care. Today, it simply meant that he and Deepti could start their fling a few hours sooner than planned without a stressful meeting with his parents to contend with.

Hoisting Bella on to his shoulders, they walked through beautiful, manicured gardens before reaching the Nature Playground. Bella laughed with delight as she explored the tunnels of the Magical Woods and climbed Log Valley.

He adored spending the time with the children; it was one of the highlights of his days. When he'd initially agreed to accompany them to Singapore, he'd expected to hand them over without any problems. Now, he wasn't looking forward to saying goodbye. He would miss them so much. He was still satisfied his parents were the best guardians for Bella and Leo since, as retirees, they could be there for the children. But he would keep in regular contact and find time to visit Bella and Leo whenever he could.

They spent a few hours in the Nature Playground then took a look at the Butterfly Garden before his parents' car came to collect Tracey and the children. Once they had driven off, he turned to face Deepti.

'Well,' she said, twisting her hands in the front of her T-shirt. 'What now?' She glanced at him from under her eyelashes, a gesture he was sure she was making from nerves, but which he found surprisingly seductive.

Tempted as he was to rush her back to the hotel and into his bed, he reached for patience. It was her first time in Singapore and, without the children, he was sure she would want to explore the country.

'Would you like to get something to eat?' he

asked. 'Or is there somewhere specific you'd like to go?'

Deepti didn't answer immediately. He got the impression she was weighing up options in her mind.

'There's so much to see in Singapore,' she said. 'But, actually, can we go to the hotel? Your parents said they'd arrange to send my luggage there and I want to make sure everything's okay. I'd like to freshen up before we go anywhere.' She looked down at her top which had the evidence she'd spent the day with sticky hands.

During the drive to the hotel, Deepti chatted about everything she wanted to see and do on what she called her 'touristy to-do list'. He couldn't hide his smile at her attempt to ignore the heightened tension between them. He leaned forward to brush her lips with his, intending it to be a light touch, but she put her hand behind his head, deepening their kiss, testing every ounce of his resolve not to get her into bed the moment they were at the hotel room.

When the were finally checked in, Matteo opened the door to Deepti's room and waited for her to enter ahead of him. He furrowed his brows as he looked around. Perhaps he should have organised a suite for her too. It was a pretty basic room with a king-size bed he was deliberately keeping his attention off, a large three-seater sofa he was also keeping his attention off and a desk. Immediately his mind conjured an image of Deepti hoisted onto the desk with her legs wrapped round him.

He cleared his throat and walked over to join Deepti by the window. The view of Singapore's cityscape on this floor probably wasn't as good as from his suite but it seemed to be absorbing her attention. Was his presence making her uncomfortable?

'Shall I leave you to freshen up?' he said. He gave her his room number. 'You can call me when you're ready or come up.'

She gave him an absent nod.

'Is something wrong, Deepti?'

'Nothing's wrong. It's just…' She straightened her shoulders. 'When I told your parents I wanted to stay at the hotel with you, I was trying to tell you I agree to the fling.'

Matteo laughed heartily. 'I understood.' He walked over to her and drew her into his arms. 'And I'm very happy.'

'Then why did you get me this room?' she asked, her confusion evident.

Matteo grasped both hands in his and drew them to his lips, kissing one after the other.

'I want you to have your own space if you want it. I hope we send our time together, but I don't ever want you to feel you have to be with me if you want some peace or you're not in the mood.'

Deepti quirked an eyebrow.

'For company,' he added hastily.

He bent to kiss her, intending it to be light and quick, but the sensation of her soft lips pressing back created a hunger and his mouth moved urgently over hers, demanding, and receiving, a reciprocal passion.

Reluctantly, he pulled away. 'I'll leave you to freshen up.'

Deepti grabbed his hand. 'No point freshening up yet,' she muttered as she started fiddling with his shirt buttons.

Matteo suddenly forgot how to breathe. He'd imagined wining and dining Deepti, followed by a slow, sweet seduction, but she always threw out his well laid plans with even better ideas of her own.

He lifted her off her feet. She automatically wrapped her legs round his waist, bending her head to meet his eager mouth. He carried her over and placed her on the bed. She kept him cradled between her thighs as her hands went to his shirt, nimbly undoing the remaining buttons.

He wanted this. He wanted this more than he ever remembered wanting something before. But he knew what would happen if he made love to her then—he would never leave the bed. The most Deepti would get to see of Singapore was the hotel and the most she would get to sample of the cuisine was room service.

He gathered both her hands in his. Taking deep breaths to calm his racing pulse, he said, 'We need to stop.'

Deepti went very still. 'Not again! Why?'

He explained his concerns.

'I see,' she said. She rested back on her elbows. Then with a cheeky grin she grabbed the bottom of her T-shirt and pulled it over her head. 'I'm not in the mood to go sightseeing right now...'

She undid the button on her shorts. His mouth ran dry and he swallowed convulsively. He'd known how passionate she could be from her previous responses to him but he'd never expected this assertive sexuality. He was a lucky man.

'Don't let me stop you going, though,' she said, looking up at him through her drooping eyelashes. 'I'm just going to stay here. On this incredibly comfortable and reassuringly firm bed.'

When she slowly reached behind her to unclasp her bra, he growled and stalked towards her, halting her. He fully intended to unwrap the rest of this gift himself.

He knew when he was beaten, and this was a fight he was happy not to win.

# CHAPTER FIFTEEN

THE NEXT DAY, Deepti was sitting in a restaurant staring out at the view of Marina Bay. She'd been so enthralled by the architectural splendour of the Helix Bridge with its steel and glass arches that she hadn't noticed Matteo was twenty minutes late until a waiter came to take her order for the third time.

She fiddled with her phone. Should she send him a text, letting him know it was fine if he couldn't make it? She wanted him to know that she had no expectations of the fling—she didn't need him to cut short meetings or change business plans to spend time with her.

She put her phone back down. It had only been twenty minutes. If she texted him now, she could appear impatient and, since he couldn't read tone from a text, her message could come across as passive aggressive.

In thirty minutes, she would leave and buy some street food. She wanted to spend time with

Matteo, naturally, but there was still a lot of Singapore she wanted to explore. She was happy to stare out of the window for a while longer, as it would give her a chance to think through what she should do about Bella.

That morning had not started well. When she'd arrived at Matteo's parents' house, Bella had refused to come out of her room or talk to anyone until she'd heard Deepti was waiting for her in the foyer. Her grandparents had been at their wits' end, desperate for some reassurance that things would get better.

In the end Deepti had persuaded the children and grandparents to spend the morning at Marine Cove Playground. Although Bella had been enjoying herself, the adults had initially clearly been tense, watching for any negative reaction from her. But, by the time she'd finished playing, there had been a subtle shift in Bella's attitude towards her grandparents. She still wouldn't speak to them but she'd listened to them when they'd explained what was around and she'd accepted food from them.

Having no end date for Deepti being around wasn't helping Bella settle in. The little girl would keep expecting Deepti to go round. Deepti decided to book her flight home for the end of the week. That would give Matteo's parents a definitive deadline for the transition.

She really wanted Bella to be happy with her grandparents but there was no denying she would miss the little girl once she left. Perhaps she could speak to Bella's grandparents about keeping in touch, or at least occasionally hearing how Bella was doing.

Not only was she not looking forward to saying goodbye to Bella, but she also wasn't looking forward to ending her time with Matteo. But it was better if it happened sooner, when they were enjoying their brief moments together and she could remember it was only a fling, rather than later, when she would fall more deeply for him than she already had.

'Sorry I'm late,' Matteo said as he came up to their table. Deepti's eyes widened when he pressed a kiss on her lips before sitting down. In any other circumstance, it would be a typical gesture between a dating couple. But they weren't dating. She didn't really know what they were.

'Are your meetings going well?' she asked.

'As well as can be expected. The usual last-minute attempts at renegotiation. A few meetings that I probably didn't need to be involved in.'

Deepti grinned, 'I guess it's hard to relinquish control when the company's your baby.' Her smile faltered as Matteo's face became a stone mask. She hurriedly changed the topic of conversation. 'Have you been here before? The view is amazing.'

They continued to talk about non-contentious topics as they ordered and waited for their food to arrive.

After she'd finished eating her entree, she looked up from her plate to see Matteo with a broad grin.

'What?' she asked. 'Do I have sauce on my face?'

'No. It looks like you were hungry?'

She saw that he still had half his meal left.

'I guess I'm not much of a conversationalist when there's food around.'

He grinned again. 'I had noticed. When we had lunch for the first time together in Fiore, you let me talk for the majority of the meal. You only started chatting once we were on dessert.'

Heat flared in her cheeks. 'Sorry, I didn't mean to be rude.'

Matteo pressed his lips together. 'That's not what I meant at all.'

Deepti didn't respond but turned to stare out of the window instead. She sensed Matteo continue to stare at her for a few moments before he started eating again.

Matteo didn't say anything more. After he finished eating his main course, he excused himself to make a call. When he returned to the table, he asked if she wanted a dessert. When she refused, Matteo signalled for and paid the bill and they both stood up ready to leave.

Meeting for lunch was turning out to have been a really bad idea. When they'd spent time together before, she'd been Bella's companion. There might have been an attraction between them but they hadn't acted on it.

Now that they'd started this fling, things were different. A meal in their hotel room made sense, as they'd had the previous evening, but eating out for lunch was too much like dating.

And they weren't dating. They weren't at the beginning or the discovery stages of a new relationship. What they had would be over in a matter of days. She took a deep, shuddering breath at the stark reminder of what having a fling meant.

'Have you decided where you want to go this afternoon?' Matteo asked as they left the restaurant. He reached for her hand.

The previous evening, when they'd finally left her hotel room and gone to Suntec City to watch the laser show at the Fountain of Wealth, it had felt natural walking hand in hand, or with their arms around each other. But today it felt wrong. Too little compared to what she really wanted.

She pulled her hand away under the guise of taking out her phone and scrolling through the list of places she wanted to see, trying to decide where to spend her afternoon.

'Yeah, I thought I'd start with Merlion Park, because I have to see the Merlion. It is the national personification of Singapore, of course.'

'Of course,' Matteo repeated with a serious expression, teasing her as she read off her list.

She gave him a poke in the ribs then continued, 'After that, I think I'll go to Gardens by the Bay to see the flower dome, and I must see the super-trees. I've seen the photos and I still can't comprehend what they're like.'

'Good choice.'

'You've been?'

He nodded. 'Shall we go?'

She blinked, 'Pardon? Aren't you waiting for your car to be brought around?'

Matteo smiled, then reached out for her hand again, bringing it up to his mouth for a kiss. 'No, I'm coming with you. I've taken the afternoon off.'

'What?' she asked in astonishment. 'I thought you had loads of meeting today.'

'Jack is rearranging things. This past month has shown me I don't need to be at every meeting, so I'm going to delegate. There's no time to lose. There's so much for me to show you.'

Deepti wanted to cry. Every time she steeled herself to accept scraps of Matteo's attention, he showed her how caring and attentive he could be, making her long to ask for a future together. To ask for the impossible.

She was trying so hard to live for the moment, but that had never been her personality. She was the kind of person who liked to make plans for her future, lead with her head. She'd been determined not to waste their limited time together wishing things could be different but to enjoy the moments while she could. Now her heart was moving her into dangerous territory.

'I'm going to organise my return flight for the end of the week,' she said, needing to voice the definitive end of their fling.

Matteo paused and turned her to face him. 'When did you decide that?'

'This morning.' She explained her need to give a final date to help with Bella's transition. She didn't mention her own need to put an end date to this fling. A time when she would know it was over for good.

'I see. If you have any problems arranging your flight, Jack can help you.'

Deepti forced out a long breath. She hadn't expected him to fall on his knees and beg her to stay for longer, but obviously she'd hoped for a slightly bigger reaction to her announcement than that.

* * *

Having waited until he could find a secluded spot as they went along the Changi Coastal Walk, Matteo groaned when Deepti broke their kiss and pushed him away from her. He grabbed her round the waist and pulled her back into him, making her squeal. If only there was a bed nearby: he wanted her beneath him.

'Matteo, people can see you.'

He looked around him at the other visitors along the boardwalk.

'Let them,' he said, cupping her face in his hands and covering her mouth with his She actively participated in their kiss for a few moments then pulled and tried to get away a second time. When he went to grab her again, she giggled and swerved out of his reach.

'Come on, Matteo. We still have lots to see before we need to leave for your parents. Here—you can hold my hand,' she said, putting hers out for him.

Matteo made a face, which made her laugh, but he enveloped her slim hand in both of his. Not for the first time, he was regretting his resolution to make sure Deepti didn't miss out on seeing everything on her 'touristy to-do list'.

Over the past couple of days, they'd visited museums, galleries and more gardens. Watching Deepti's expressions had been more interesting to him than the attractions themselves, although seeing the places through Deepti's eyes, like at the waterfall, was like seeing them for the first time.

That morning they'd woken up early to go to Mount Faber Park so they could watch the sunrise together before he went to his office. Each of those moments with her took his breath away.

And at all of these places, apart from the Buddha Tooth Relic Temple, he sought out quiet, private areas where he could give in to his urge to kiss her until she was as breathless as he felt.

He had never been prone to public displays of affection before; at most his dates got his elbow as support when he was escorting them round. With Deepti, he hadn't been able to resist, taking every opportunity to sneak a kiss.

'We could be late for my parents,' he said, as they continued to walk. 'We could go back to the hotel first.'

She paused, biting her lip. He grinned. He loved that she was seriously thinking about his suggestion. She had thrown herself wholeheartedly into their fling, meeting his passion with an intensity of her own. His face fell when she shook her head.

'No, we can't be late. I promised Bella we'd be round a bit earlier today. And I don't want to have to come up with two believable excuses to give your parents for our lateness, particularly why we're both late and arriving exactly at the same time.'

'Then tell them the truth. You can say we're late because I was having my wicked way with you,' he replied, pulling her back to him and wrapping his arms around her.

'Matteo,' she said, using the stern tone he'd got used to whenever he'd sneaked kisses from her when they'd been with Bella or his parents.

He was going to miss that tone when she was gone…in only a few days. He went still. It didn't matter how much fun he had been having, they'd made an agreement that it would end once she left Singapore. He turned away from her.

If Deepti was surprised by his sudden change of mood, she didn't say anything but, as they continued walking, she would gaze over at him, her expression a mix of understanding and resignation.

They had spent an idyllic few days since arriving in Singapore. He'd visited Bella every evening with Deepti. What his parents thought about them arriving and leaving together, he didn't really care, as long as they didn't make Deepti feel uncomfortable in any way.

Deepti always joined his parents for a drink after putting Bella to bed, in a similar way to the

updates she used to give him. His lips quirked.
He was certain his parents didn't have the same
ulterior motive he'd had.

So far, they had refused his parents' invita-
tions to stay for dinner, but he knew he a proper
conversation with them was long overdue. He
didn't mind if Deepti was part of the conversation—in fact he would prefer it—but he knew
his parents wouldn't be comfortable discussing
family truths in front of someone they considered a stranger.

In some ways, since they'd only known each
other for a month, Deepti was still a stranger
to him. But she was someone he had wanted
to get to know better almost from the first moment he'd met her. In another world, they probably wouldn't be ending their fling so soon,
but they'd set out the parameters at the beginning. He couldn't ask her to change them now…
could he?

Deepti had booked her return to England. The
date coincided with his departure for Dubai.
What would Deepti think if he asked her to go
to Dubai with him so they could spend a few
more days together? It was a tempting thought.
But was there really any point when they would
simply be prolonging the inevitable?

But they had agreed it was a fling, and Deepti
had never brought up the idea of continuing their

relationship back in England. In fact, Deepti had made it quite clear that she wanted nothing to do with him once it had ended—she'd not even shared her plans for getting a job. He was tempted to offer help finding her a position to tide her over, something he had never offered anyone before, and something he had never previously considered before.

But one week was too short, even for a fling. He employed extremely competent people who could easily carry out the work he kept taking on himself. In fact, his business was at the stage where he could step back and take on a caretaker role, perhaps even look for a new venture—maybe take the yacht and sail round the world. Perhaps he would bring up extending her stay once they left his parents.

The evening with Bella went well and it was looking increasingly as if there would be no need for Deepti to delay her return on Bella's account. So, the only option was to ask Deepti to delay her return on his account.

He brought it up later that evening when they were taking a walk along the bay before dinner. She let her hand fall out of his and stopped walking.

'Why?' she asked.

He frowned. She wasn't exactly leaping up

and down with joy at the prospect of extending their fling.

'If you still don't have to rush home, I could show you some places in Dubai we didn't get a chance to see on the way up, and then we can take the yacht to Egypt.'

'I've already booked my return,' she replied.

'That's not a problem,' he said. He could organise the changes to her airline ticket. If necessary, he could charter a private jet to get her to England. In which case, he could probably go back with her.

'It's a bit out of the blue.'

He rubbed his neck. She was going to turn him down but hadn't definitely said no yet. He turned to look at the water. It didn't matter if she didn't want to continue their fling. It had always been time-limited. The more time they spent together, the greater the risk she would develop feelings for him.

He'd already made major changes to his schedule and plans to fit in more time with her. If he let it continue, then she would keep trying to burrow her way into his heart, and he wasn't going to let that happen. He would always be grateful to her that she had helped him have a relationship with his nephew and niece. And the doors of a relationship with his parents were ajar. But he didn't do love and he didn't do romantic emotions.

'It does make more sense for you to keep with your timetable,' he said curtly.

Deepti laughed. 'Have you changed your mind already?'

He tilted his head. 'What?' She was keeping him off-kilter and he didn't like it.

'Are you un-inviting me from Dubai?' She was still smiling but it didn't reach her eyes and he couldn't read the emotion behind it.

'Of course not. I would love you to join me,' he said, simply and honestly. 'There is no pressure. If you've already started making arrangements for when you're back home, then I completely understand that you don't want to make any last-minute changes.'

She expelled a breath like a sigh. And she had the same slightly lost, slightly hurt expression as always when the subject of her plans back home came up. He wanted to offer to help with whatever problem she was facing. He wanted her to know he was on her side.

But that wasn't part of their agreement. He wasn't her partner. He wasn't even her boyfriend. After this fling ended, they would be nothing to each other.

# CHAPTER SIXTEEN

DEEPTI PUT DOWN the book she was trying to read and then stretched out on the sofa area of the guest-floor deck. She couldn't really concentrate anyway and was feeling at a bit of a loose end. They'd been back on board the yacht for three days.

In the end, rather than fly to Dubai and join the yacht there, Matteo had decided to sail to Dubai.

Before she'd agreed to extend their fling, they'd considered the impact delaying her departure could have on Bella. Since Matteo knew Deepti well enough to know there was no chance of her staying in Singapore and not spending time with Bella, they'd decided she would leave on her planned date. Instead, Matteo changed his arrangements.

It was odd being back on *Serendipity* and not spending the day with Bella. Saying goodbye to her had been even harder than she'd expected.

Even though it had only been a few weeks, she'd grown very attached to the young girl which, based on her previous limited experience with children, was something she would never have expected when she'd first agreed to be Bella's companion.

If Deepti had this much trouble saying goodbye to Bella, how badly would it hurt to say goodbye to Matteo when the time finally came? And, unlike with Bella, Deepti doubted he'd agree to have video chats with her so they could keep in touch.

In the end, it hadn't been difficult to agree to his offer to extend their fling, even if it was only for a few more days. And this time she knew the reason wasn't because she was putting off returning to England. She liked Matteo, loved being in his company. She wanted to spend as much time with him as possible before they had to part for good. Soon all she would have would be her memories and she was determined to make as many as possible.

Matteo had suggested she move into his suite of rooms, but she asked to stay in her former bedroom. Sharing a room, even for the few days it would take to reach Dubai, would have been too much like a real relationship—and she needed to constantly remind herself they were having a fling. It was easier to protect her feelings if she had a separate room like she'd had in the hotel.

They had less than seven days left together. She was going to make every one of them count. But she was absolutely determined not to delay her return to England once they reached Dubai. Not only did she have to start putting the pieces of her life back together, but she also had to protect her heart.

And, the closer she became to Matteo, the stronger grew the feeling of guilt that she was lying to him, and that didn't sit well with her at all. Particularly when Matteo had been open and honest with her about how he'd been betrayed in the worst possible way.

It made complete sense that he found it difficult to trust people, especially on a personal level. But she wanted him to trust her. And how could she expect that when she had been hiding the truth about her past and her future? Was there any really good reason to hide it?

Although they had only known each other for such a short time, in many ways Matteo already knew her better than anyone else did. She had to believe he knew her well enough to know she would never have betrayed someone's trust, not on a personal or professional level.

Their fling would soon be over, and she could save herself the potential hurt if the conversation didn't go the way she planned, but she wanted him to know the truth. She didn't want there to be any secrets between them, on her part. She wanted him to know he could trust her—as she, against all odds, had learnt to trust him.

It was all very well in theory to make the decision to tell him the truth, but how did she bring up something like that? Perhaps after dinner, when they were sitting out on the deck, sharing a glass of wine in the hot tub.

She imagined how that conversation could go.

*Oh, by the way, Matteo, I actually work in the financial sector and I know a lot about your business and the kind of deals you've been working on. I joined the crew of the* Serendipity *when I was fired from my job because I didn't land an important deal. And I also lost a very important client for the firm, losing it millions in income.*

*But there's more. The deal and the client went to the company belonging to my boyfriend at the time so, while some of the people I worked for think I'm merely incompetent, the majority think I'm corrupt and unethical because I purposely let my boyfriend take the deal.*

Even thinking it made her head hurt.

Before, during or after a meal didn't feel like the right time, but at the same time she couldn't really make an appointment through Jack to tell Matteo the truth.

She decided to find Alex to ask his opinion. She didn't know whether it was because she was distracted, or muscle memory from her visits to Matteo made her go to the foyer rather than take the crew stairs, but she realised her error when the guest waiting by the lift turned when he heard her approach.

She froze on the spot. She had been so careful to avoid seeing any guests and, the one time she made a mistake, she bumped into someone she knew. Not just knew—someone whose company was a client of her firm.

'Deepti, I thought I'd seen you sitting out on the deck. What a surprise!'

'Mr Partlin. How nice to bump into you. How have you been?' Deepti's mind frantically worked through the potential repercussions of this meeting and whether Mr Partlin was likely to mention it to Matteo.

'Good, good. Are you here for meetings with Mr Di Corrado too?'

She shook her head.

'Oh, do you work for him now? To be honest, I was a bit disappointed when your colleague contacted me a few months ago to let me know you were leaving the company. I would have hoped you valued me as a client to let me know personally. Then I heard you'd been let go as part of a restructuring, so I was confused.'

Deepti narrowed her eyes. 'One of my colleagues contacted you a few months ago about me leaving?'

'Yes, maybe three or four months ago. They told me you were leaving and your clients would be redistributed.'

Deepti couldn't believe what she was hearing. She'd been let go only two months ago but someone had contacted her clients well before then about her departure. Who would have done that…and why? It sounded as if what had happened with her work hadn't been a simple scenario of someone taking advantage of the situation, but that someone had perhaps engineered the situation and planned it in advance. This could be her first major breakthrough in trying to clear her name.

'Mr Partlin, can you tell me more about this, please? It's important…'

It felt like ages since Matteo had spent some time alone with Deepti, or seen her at all. She refused to join him for meals while he had guests on board, saying it didn't make sense having to give the people explanations for her presence.

He wondered whether he could spend time with her in her room later that evening, after he'd socialised with his guests for a short while after dinner—as short a time as possible. But it would still be fairly late. Matteo didn't want to turn up uninvited at night so he decided he should check with her in advance. In theory, he could send her a text, but that felt so impersonal at this stage. It wouldn't take him more than five minutes to pop down to her level and see her in person, perhaps hold her in his arms for a brief while.

If only his next meeting didn't involve a video conference with other countries—he could have asked his guests to delay their meeting. But, the quicker he got down to Deepti's deck, the more time he would have to spend with her.

He took the first couple of flights two steps at a time but slowed down when he heard his guest's voice coming up the stairwell.

'I need to prepare for my meeting, but it was a treat bumping into you here. If I can do anything to help you, let me know, Deepti.'

'No, you've already done more than you'll ever realise Mr Partlin,' Deepti said.

Matteo frowned. It didn't sound like the conversation of two people who had just met on board the yacht. How did they know each other?

'And don't worry, Deepti. I understand and I won't say anything to Mr Di Corrado about what happened.'

Hearing that, Matteo made his presence known. 'Won't say anything to me about what?'

Mr Partlin put a comforting hand on Deepti's arm. 'I'm sorry, Deepti.'

Matteo watched a slideshow of emotions cross Deepti's face. The overwhelming one was guilt. She'd been hiding something from him.

His mind immediately went to the idea the two had been having an affair but, despite his experience with his ex-fiancée, nothing Deepti had done would suggest she had another lover.

Or was he deluding himself? He would never have suspected his ex-fiancée was cheating on him but she had been. He kept his tone even when he turned to Mr Partlin and asked, 'How do you know Deepti?'

Partlin looked reluctant to answer before finally saying, 'My company is a client of her firm and Deepti was our relationship manager.'

Matteo didn't miss Deepti's sharp intake of breath.

'It was a purely business relationship,' Mr Partlin added hastily, his eyes darting from Matteo to Deepti.

'Can we please talk, Matteo?' Deepti asked.

He ignored her pleading expression and said, 'Mr Partlin, we should get back to our meeting. The others are probably waiting on video conference.' He gestured for his guest to go ahead of him.

'I'll speak to you later, Matteo,' Deepti said, putting her hand on his arm.

He pressed his lips together, not trusting himself to speak, and, shaking off her hand, he went upstairs without responding.

It was almost impossible to concentrate on the negotiations when he kept replaying the brief conversation he'd overheard.

So Deepti had had a previous career in finance. Why had she kept that hidden from him? Was it purely a coincidence that she was on the yacht?

He couldn't help recalling his initial suspicions that Deepti had engineered things to get closer to him. He'd put those doubts to the side quickly after spending time with her, even making excuses for why she was being evasive about her past. Now, it was starting to make more sense. Had he been right about her in the first place?

How much of what she'd said to him was the truth? Was she really a pastry chef with a *cordon bleu* qualification? She'd admitted she'd never crewed before and had also told him she had no restaurant experience. He couldn't see any reason why she would lie about that. So why would someone who'd had a previous career in the financial sector choose to crew on his yacht? Unless it was part of a scheme to get close to him.

He wanted to ask Mr Partlin more details but, from what he'd overheard, the man wouldn't tell him anything that Deepti didn't want him to know. He could ask her for an explanation but how much of what she said to him could he believe now? How could he ever trust anything she said to him again?

'Matteo? Matteo, do you need to take a break?' his executive assistant asked him over video, interrupting his deliberations on Deepti.

He waved a hand. 'No, let's continue,' he replied.

With a deliberate exertion of will power, he purposely put all thoughts of Deepti to the back of his mind until after dinner, when he sent her a text asking her to come to his office. He intentionally selected his office because he wanted... he needed...to keep a clear head for the conversation they needed to have. He knew himself well enough to know that was less likely to happen in a room with a bed or sofa.

Deepti had her fists clenched and her shoulders were tense when she entered the room. He pressed his lips together to resist offering her some comfort. Instead, he pointed her to the chair on the opposite side of his desk.

'Matteo, I…' she began.

He put up a hand to stop her. 'You lied to me about previous work.'

'I didn't lie. I just never told you the whole truth.'

The disappointment in her response was almost visceral.

'Don't play semantics with me. Why did you lie about your qualifications? You don't even need to have culinary qualifications to work as crew chef.'

She stiffened. 'I wasn't lying about that. I do have a *cordon bleu* certificate in pastry. That's why Alex offered me the position. But it is true he is the only reason I got it. I never crewed before.'

'You worked in the financial profession but you also have a *cordon bleu* pastry qualification. Do you know how unlikely that sounds?'

She put both palms up in a gesture of surrender.

'It's a long story,' she said with a small, weak smile.

His heart twisted at the sorrow behind her eyes. He steeled himself not to react, not to feel sympathy. Not to feel anything. 'I don't want to hear it.' He paused. There was too much he didn't understand and he didn't like the way that made him feel. 'Why did you hide your previous job?'

'I was embarrassed.'

'Explain,' he demanded.

His worst fears were realised when Deepti told him about having failed to land a deal and losing an important client. That she would grab the opportunity to work on his boat all made sense. If she'd landed him as a client, he would have been the perfect person to help her get back into her field. She must have counted her blessings when Bella had formed an attachment to her and he'd practically begged her to be Bella's companion. Was that the real reason she'd persuaded him to spend time with Bella too—so she could get closer to him?

Or was there something more sinister behind her presence on his yacht? Had she, perhaps deliberately, joined the crew so she could find out details of his guests and exploit that information for monetary gain? She had access to the details of all the guests who came to the yacht. Coming from the financial field, she would understand exactly what kind of deals he could be working on.

He bit out the accusation, watching closely for her reaction.

'What?' She flinched, blinking rapidly. Her surprise seemed genuine, but she could be an excellent actress. She'd certainly fooled him with her feigned vulnerable openness.

'There has to be a reason you joined the crew.'

'I told you, I needed to get away for a few weeks to regroup.'

'Why should I believe anything you say?'

'You know me.'

'No, I don't. I don't know anything about you.'

Her sharp exhalation showed him his comment had hurt her. But he couldn't care about that. He didn't care about the fact she'd got fired. He didn't even care that she might have colluded with her boyfriend. He cared that she had hidden her past. He only cared about her lies.

For the first time in years, he'd opened up to someone new. He'd started to believe that he could trust someone, maybe even have a real relationship. Instead, he felt the same sense of betrayal he'd felt when Luca and Lauren had told him about their relationship. In an odd way, it felt worse.

'The helicopter will be here tomorrow morning. You need to be on it. Leave.'

# CHAPTER SEVENTEEN

DEEPTI SAT ON a lounger wrapped in a blanket, watching the sun come out over the horizon. Jack had messaged to say the helicopter would be ready in a couple of hours.

She stretched. Her body wanted the rest her mind had denied her all night. She felt broken and bruised. But she refused to give into the tears pricking behind her eyelids.

Why hadn't she told Matteo the truth sooner, when he'd first asked her about job experience all those weeks ago? Nothing in her rationale made any sense, looking back at it.

Would it have made any difference if Matteo hadn't overheard her conversation with Mr Partlin? He would never believe that she had planned to tell him the truth that very day. She couldn't blame him. But he hadn't believed anything she had to say. He'd even accused her of something far worse than any reason she'd come up with for hiding the truth. Why couldn't he see that his accusation didn't even make any sense? She had gone out of her way to avoid any talk about business—why would she do that if the only reason for her to get close to him was to get information about possible deals?

Perhaps, once Matteo had calmed down, he would realise he was being unfair and there was no basis to that allegation.

She straightened her shoulders and tossed her head back.

It didn't matter. The fact he could accuse her of that demonstrated more clearly than if he had said out loud he believed she was guilty of having acted unethically. What kind of person did he believe she must be to not only come up with a plan to get close to him for her career but also to have a physical relationship with him for that reason?

Accepting the cold, stark reality that she'd developed feelings for someone who didn't know her at all hurt more than she'd thought it would. She'd slowly started to trust someone again only to find out he didn't believe in her.

She heard footsteps behind her. A glimmer of hope ignited that it could be Matteo. She swivelled her head, the hope being dashed when she saw Alex holding a plate of food.

'Morning, Dee,' Alex said. 'You didn't come to the mess for dinner yesterday and I know you didn't eat with the guests. I thought you might be hungry.'

She shook her head. 'I'm okay.'

'Jack said you're going on the helicopter.'

She nodded. 'Matteo has asked me to leave. I'm going to leave.'

'Why, though? You looked so good together, so comfortable. Everyone at the pub mentioned it. Nobody was surprised to hear he'd invited you back on the *Serendipity*.'

'It was just a fling. And now it's over.'

'Do you want to talk about it?'

'What's there to talk about? He found out I used to be a relationship manager for an investment company. That was bad enough of a deception for him. But he also knows I was fired, and now he thinks the only reason I took this job and spent time with him is because I was trying to use him to restart my career.'

Alex's jaw dropped. 'What?' he asked, with a disbelieving laugh. 'How can he even think that? Doesn't he know you at all?'

'Apparently not.' She shook her head, pressing her lips together, the pricking behind her eyes getting harder to control. 'Maybe I should have told him the truth from the start.'

Alex shrugged but his expression told her that was what he would have done.

'But was it such a bad thing to not tell him,'

she said, twisting her hands. 'It didn't affect being Bella's companion. And I didn't have anything to do with his guests or business deals.'

'Of course you didn't! But Dee, you were in a relationship. Why wouldn't you tell him?'

'Oh, I don't know. Because I never make the right decisions. I do everything wrong.' She cradled her knees, resting her head on them.

'Don't you dare speak like that, Dee. If Matteo isn't listening to you and offering you support, then he doesn't deserve you.'

She straightened. She wanted to believe Alex was right.

Anger and irritation began to rise up in her, warring against the pain and hurt. What had she done that was so wrong? She hadn't told him about her past job because she didn't want him judging her like all the others had; because she'd been humiliated by her ex-boyfriend's actions; because she wanted to exist in a cocoon where the past didn't matter.

She hadn't told him because she'd been worried he wouldn't believe in her innocence. A worry that had been proved well-founded, as it turned out. How dared he doubt her innocence? Now, like then, she hadn't done anything wrong. She'd worked hard to get her *cordon bleu* qualification. He couldn't belittle that achievement. And, if he didn't believe her, he didn't believe

Alex, and she wasn't going to let anyone question her friend's character. At least Alex had never doubted her.

Matteo had to realise she couldn't have conjured up Bella's attachment to her. Deepti's presence in Matteo's company had been a huge coincidence. Surely he would see that when he'd had a chance to think clearly, when he wasn't so busy with his guests? She just needed to find another chance to speak to him.

'I have to go, Alex. I need to find Matteo and speak to him.'

She couldn't find Matteo on the main deck and the offices were locked. She could go up to the owner's deck, but what would be the point? Since he'd never given her the code to open his door, she would simply be waiting out in the foyer, hoping he'd come out.

All the fight seeped out of her. What was the point of this? If she spoke to Matteo, if she managed to change his mind, what of it? Their fling was coming to an end anyway. Did it really matter if it ended while he still had a bad impression of her?

She understood that he had trust issues. He been betrayed in the worst possible way. But how could he think she was anything like his ex-fiancée? Why couldn't he trust her? She hadn't committed any crimes. She hadn't broken any laws. She had simply failed to disclose a painful situation from her past.

He should have trusted that she would never betray him. She'd gone out of her way to change the topic when he'd wanted to discuss work, and had asked Alex not to tell her who was on the guest list so there would be no way for her to get any information about what deals Matteo could be working on. She'd been very careful that she couldn't be accused of gathering inside information if she managed to get her financial career back.

And for her efforts to be scorned by Matteo...

She gritted her teeth.

It was exactly the kind of anger and outrage she needed to clear her name back home and get her life on track.

She was going to start with Matteo.

She heard the helicopter arriving above her head. She folded her arms across her chest. Matteo could try to avoid her all he wanted. She was going to speak to him. When the helicopter left with his guests, she wouldn't be on it.

She was gone.

The helicopter had left over an hour ago. Matteo swivelled his office chair to look out of the window.

Good. He didn't need people he couldn't trust

around him. Deepti had proved she was just like all the others—hiding things from him and using him to achieve her own ends. If he hadn't found out the truth about Deepti's background, who knew what kind of information she could have found out and shared, affecting so many potential deals?

He'd suspected as much when he'd first met her. He should have relied on his instincts then and not let his concern for Bella affect his decision making.

Thank goodness he'd only offered her a fling. He'd almost considered asking her to prolong her stay even longer. He'd almost asked her if she would continue their relationship when he got back to England.

He buzzed Jack to let him know he could have the rest of the day off.

He was in his lounge reading a financial report when Deepti appeared at the top of the stairs.

He blinked. 'I thought you'd left.'

Deepti stuck out her jaw. 'I decided not to.'

His eyes narrowed. 'I wasn't offering you a choice.'

She shrugged carelessly. 'It wasn't convenient for me to leave today.' He stared in amazement as she sat down on the sofa next to his, leaned back and rested her head in her hands.

Who was this person? Had he ever really known her?

'Not convenient?' he repeated.

'I wasn't expecting to be in Dubai today. I don't have a hotel room booked. I chose not to spend time and effort looking for a last-minute place when I can stay on this yacht and arrive in Dubai as scheduled.'

Matteo swallowed. In his anger, he'd ordered Deepti to leave, but had taken no action to make sure she would be safe and have a place to stay. He wasn't such a cold-hearted brute that he wanted her to suffer harm for her actions.

'I'll arrange accommodation and call the helicopter to come back tomorrow.'

Deepti sat up. 'Ah, I see you're still not ready to be rational. I'll come back to talk to you tomorrow evening.'

Something intense flared in him at her determination. He steeled himself not to respond.

'You won't be here tomorrow evening,' he said.

'I'm not going anywhere. Not until we've had a chance to talk properly.'

'I have nothing to say to you.'

'That's a shame, because I have plenty to say to you.'

He'd always liked her sassiness, and the way she wasn't afraid to hold her ground against him, but there was an added anger behind her words this time.

What did she have to be angry about? That he'd discovered her secret so she couldn't use him for her career?

'More lies. I'm not interested.'

'You can call it semantics, but I never lied to you.'

'Of course, you just hid the truth.'

'Yes! I hid the truth about the most humiliating, horrible thing that ever happened to me. And you're angry that I was reluctant to share it with you.'

'Yes, because I shared the worst thing that happened to me with you.'

She flinched. He closed his eyes and took a deep breath. He hadn't wanted to admit out loud the reason her deceptive behaviour hurt him so much.

'You had every opportunity to tell me, Deepti. If it was as you're claiming, a lost deal and a lost client, why wouldn't you tell me? The truth is, you were hoping to find some information about the kinds of deals I was working on. Or maybe you were hoping to get your job back by landing me as a major client. I'm sure I'd make up for the one you lost. Just admit it; there's no need for pretence. I'm not adverse to discussing the possibility.'

And he hated how that was true despite her deceit.

'You honestly believe I'm capable of using you for that?'

Matteo pressed his lips together. A muscle spasmed in his jaw. All the fight seemed to have gone out of her. He turned his face away. He sensed Deepti scrutinising him.

Without saying a word, she left.

He half-rose from his seat, then sat back down.

It was better this way.

# CHAPTER EIGHTEEN

THE FIRST TWO weeks back in London were exhausting. Deepti threw herself into the goal of clearing her name and finding a new job with an unearthly zeal. And, when she wasn't trying to clear her name or search for jobs, she was meeting up with old friends. Anything to make sure that when it was time for bed she was so bone-weary sleep came almost immediately.

Mr Partlin's comment that her colleague had contacted him gave Deepti an avenue to try, since she assumed Mr Partlin's company wouldn't be the only one they approached. While she was waiting for her contacts to get back to her, she threw herself wholeheartedly into finding another job. The number of contacts willing to meet her to discuss potential roles made it clear to Deepti that she'd overestimated the effect her firing had had on her reputation—another thing she'd got wrong.

She should have stayed in England and fought

to clear her name back when she'd first got fired instead of running away to sea with her tail between her legs. That could have saved her a lot of heartbreak.

Deepti sighed. But she would have missed out on a lot of fun, getting to know new people, exploring new places.

And Matteo. She couldn't regret that decision, even with the benefit of hindsight. Not even knowing how much she missed him—every moment of every day.

She hated how much she missed him. She should be angry with him. He'd leapt to the worst conclusion about her. Not only had he disregarded her fears and feelings of shame and inadequacy at being fired from a position she'd had for over seven years, but he'd also come up with such an outlandish reason for her presence on *Serendipity*.

Her family and friends had always been behind her. It would have been good to have Matteo's support but it was never essential.

Even though she was angry, in her heart of hearts she could also understand why he doubted her. He'd been betrayed by his brother and fiancée, and in a way his parents—how could she fail to understand why trust was a such big problem for him?

He only had her word that she'd never intended to use him for her career. To him, she was probably another person who'd used her relationship with him to get what she wanted.

The reality was, after being fired, she'd lost confidence and had started second-guessing herself in a way she'd never done before. Although she had always wanted to clear her name, without her time on the yacht she might never have been prepared to fight for it the way she had been doing since coming back.

But somehow that made it harder to accept her own responsibility for the situation she was now in. Like Matteo, she'd lost her ability to trust. She hadn't been able to trust that he would be on her side when she told him the truth and she hadn't been able to trust her own judgement.

And, more importantly, she'd hadn't trusted the way she felt about Matteo. She'd been frightened of falling too fast, too soon. She'd been frightened of being able to trust her emotions after her experience with her ex-boyfriend. She'd agreed to a fling because it was safer for her than admit that she'd fallen in love in such a short space of time.

And she'd held part of herself back during their fling because she'd believed, if she didn't completely open herself up, then it wouldn't hurt so much when their affair inevitably ended— she'd been wrong about that too.

Matteo, on the other hand, had been open with her. He'd shared his past with her. Perhaps he hadn't wanted to offer her anything more than a brief fling, but he'd shown her in a hundred different ways that he cared about her.

By protecting her heart, by keeping part of her past a secret from him, wasn't she the one who'd ensured nothing real could develop between them?

She had never told him how she felt.

How she loved him.

Why had it taken her so long to admit that? Because she hadn't trusted her own feelings. She'd been scared to admit she had fallen so quickly and so deeply.

She'd accepted a brief, time-limited affair, convincing herself that if that was all on offer she would take it. But how much of her acceptance had been due to her loss of confidence and trust in herself? She hadn't believed the feelings she had for Matteo were real. They'd come on so quickly and with such intensity—she'd never experienced anything like that before.

But the point now wasn't to live in the past and wallow in the guilt of what she hadn't done. The point now was to decide what she needed to do next.

First, she was going to sort out her career. Then she was going to go to Matteo and tell him how much she loved him. If he didn't believe anything else she told him, she would make him believe that.

For the first time in a long time, she knew exactly what she was going to do, and she was absolutely certain it was the right decision.

Matteo looked out at the view of the Manhattan skyline. It had been two weeks since Deepti had left. He bit out a sharp sigh of frustration. He needed to stop measuring time in terms of Deepti.

What was she doing now? Had she managed to sort out the problems with her last job?

It hadn't taken long for him to realise his suspicion that she'd wanted to take advantage of him for business purposes was meritless. She'd gone out of her way to avoid talk about his work and had even refused to meet his guests—not the actions of someone who wanted inside information.

And it was obvious she was bright. She didn't need to use him to get her career back on track if she put her mind to it. He was confident about that.

It was easier to believe that she was untrustworthy in business than it would be to discover, one day, that she was an untrustworthy lover.

He'd grown up with his brother. He'd been with his fiancée for a few years. He hadn't suspected a thing. Which proved he couldn't trust women. He'd had a fling with a beautiful, intelligent woman. He'd enjoyed talking to Deepti as much as he'd enjoyed sleeping with her. He enjoyed her. It had ended badly a few days early, but an ending had been inevitable.

He'd had two weeks since then to put all thoughts of her behind him. Put in context, two weeks was almost half the time they'd been together on the boat.

He gave a harsh laugh and closed his eyes. These past two weeks had dragged along, despite how many meetings he crammed in and the numerous cities he visited. In comparison, it seemed as if the time with Deepti had flown by. He'd barely spent any time with her but at the same time it felt as if he'd known her all his life.

His phone beeped, reminding him that he was due to have a video call with Bella. It took a few attempts to connect. His mother's face appeared next to Bella's.

Matteo raised his eyebrows. 'Is something wrong?' he asked.

'No, we were finishing a bedtime story from Deepti and Bella asked to read it five times. The poor dear was exhausted.'

Matteo's heart skipped, hearing Deepti's name when he'd just been thinking about her, and he damped down the impulse to ask how she was and whether she mentioned his name at all. This was his time to chat to Bella. She needed to be his focus.

Although Bella only wanted to talk about Deepti. Whenever he wasn't clear about what Bella was telling him, his mother was there to clarify. Which was how he learnt that Deepti was still looking for a job.

He thought about that after he ended the call with Bella. He didn't like thinking about Deepti struggling to find a new job. He wanted her to be happy. He ought to find a way to help her. He could put some feelers out but not have anything set in stone until Deepti said she was happy for him to go ahead.

He could introduce her to potential clients. He could even look at his personal investments. His research had highlighted that, before the incidents which had caused her to lose her job, she'd been well respected in the field and smaller companies had wanted to sign with her. His name could help open doors to some bigger companies.

He would do whatever it took to show her he had been wrong and that he trusted and believed in her completely.

He was due to stay in New York for another four days, but he didn't like the idea of Deepti suffering on her own. He contacted his executive assistant in London to discuss cancelling his meetings and returning to England. Her barely concealed surprise was understandable. He was not behaving in character at all.

'Would you like me to make an urgent appointment with your doctor? she asked, suddenly concerned.

He shook his head. 'I'm fine.' Naturally he hadn't told her about Deepti, and he had no intention of explaining himself. 'Oh, I'm also going to send you a list of people. Can you get their contact numbers and ideally line up phone calls with them over the next week?' He would get the details of people in his network who would do him a favour and help Deepti out.

'Okay, Matteo. I'll see what I can do. I'm sure I'll be able to reschedule or delegate the meetings you have set for the next few days.'

'I don't know.' Matteo paused. The Deepti he knew would not be pleased if he forged ahead, trying to sort out her career without discussing it with her first. 'In fact, get me the contact details, but put a hold on organising those meetings for now.'

'Are you sure everything is okay, Matteo?' Her concern was not unsurprising, since he'd never been this indecisive before.

He smiled to reassure her. 'I am fine. I need to sort out something in England first. Assume

I'm not available for any meetings for seventy-two hours after I get to England.'

'Seventy-two hours?' The high-pitched incredulity in her tone made Matteo's lips quirk.

'At least seventy-two. In fact, instead of rescheduling my meetings, delegate them all.' Travelling on the yacht had shown him a different pace of life. He wasn't the only person who could handle everything that came up in his business. 'If they can't be delegated, cancel them. I'm going to take a holiday. For two weeks.'

'You're taking a holiday? For two weeks?'

He was in danger of his executive assistant sending him for medical evaluation at this rate. He threw her a bone.

'I need to see someone and sort things out. I don't know how long that's going to take. But that's the priority.'

His executive assistant grinned. 'No, that's absolutely fine. I will take care of everything. I'll get you on the first flight out tomorrow morning, unless you want to charter a private jet.'

'Tomorrow will be fine.'

'Perfect. Leave everything to me. And Mattco?'

'Yes?'

'I hope everything works out with Deepti,' she said as she ended the call.

His jaw dropped, then he laughed. He shouldn't

be surprised that his executive assistant knew about Deepti. She knew everything that was going on. He only hoped he could introduce them one day; they would get on like a house on fire.

He sat back and swivelled his seat towards the skyline view.

Yes, Deepti was important to him. He wanted to see her. Would she agree to see him after the way he'd behaved? He'd overreacted to her confession because it had been easier to convince himself she was just another woman who couldn't be trusted than one day face the possibility that she would betray him, as his fiancée had.

But he knew, beyond a shadow of a doubt, Deepti would never do that. He'd been upset by her lack of faith in him; that she hadn't felt secure enough in *them* to share such an important situation with him. But the only reason she'd had the power to evoke that reaction from him was because of the way he felt about her. She was able to hurt him deeply because he had already developed a strong and deep affection for her.

It was so different from the way he had felt about Lauren. When he'd found out about Luca's and Lauren's relationship, it was his brother's betrayal that had hurt him more, and that should have told him everything. But in his anger and hurt he had made himself believe Lauren was the love of his life who his brother had stolen from him.

The reality was he had proposed to Lauren because they had been together for two years and he'd felt it was the right step to take. They had already started to grow apart soon after he'd proposed, and his loss of interest had made her become an after-thought in the busy-ness of building up his business. In all his brief flings since then, his dates had always been after-thoughts too.

Until Deepti. Deepti was always his first thought, if not his every thought. He *needed* to see to her. Not only to help her sort out her career. And not only to tell her he was sorry he'd doubted her, although he prayed she would accept his apology.

He wanted to tell her he loved her. Because he did.

He knew she had helped him open his heart to Bella and Leo, but it was only now dawning on him that he'd been able to do that because he'd started opening his heart to her too. Probably from the first day they'd met when she'd been covered in flour but still the most beautiful person he'd ever seen. Her humour and kind-ness had shone through.

He would give anything for a chance to be

with her and hoped that one day she would learn to love him too.

And he would never give her cause to doubt whether he loved her or whether she was the most important thing in his life because he would show her every day.

But first he had to get to see her in England and hope she didn't slam the door in this face.

# CHAPTER NINETEEN

IN THE END, it had been surprisingly easy to clear her name, Deepti reflected a week later. As she suspected, she could have sorted this situation out almost immediately if she'd had confidence in herself and trusted her own judgement.

Once it had been made clear that she hadn't been involved in the collapse of the deal or the loss of the client, her old employer had asked her to return, but Deepti had been firm that she needed to move forward, not take a backward step. Instead, she had accepted a new position with a smaller start-up company which would use her skills in a different, more challenging way.

But the job wouldn't start for another month so that left the last item on her list—Matteo.

If only sorting things out with him would be so easy. Matteo had made it clear to her that they would never have anything more than a short fling. It would have been over in a matter of days even if he hadn't ended it early. If she tried to contact him, would that be going backwards? This wasn't the first time one of her relationships had ended, and those ones had lasted a lot longer.

Deepti sighed, knowing it wasn't about going backwards or longevity. The intensity of her feelings and the sense of being complete when she was with Matteo wasn't something that came easily. And loving him wasn't something that would go easily, either.

When she'd first left *Serendipity*, she'd kept waiting for reason and rational thought to kick in and show her that it had only been the close proximity of being on the yacht with Matteo that had led her to develop such intense feelings for him.

But now she was ignoring those doubts and listening to her heart instead. And her heart was telling her Matteo was the love of her life. Openly admitting she loved him was liberating. But it wasn't enough, and it wouldn't be until she was able to tell Matteo how she felt.

How would he react? Putting aside the fact he didn't believe her reasons why she'd hidden the truth about her job, he'd made it very clear that he wasn't prepared to, and couldn't, offer her a real relationship.

All Matteo had wanted was a fling and, now that it was over, did she ever cross his mind? She was still scared. But she was going to gather up all her reserves and believe in herself—believe in her feelings.

The difficult part would be getting to speak to Matteo in the first place. She didn't know his home address. She didn't even know which country he was in right now. Tracey didn't have any information, even though Matteo was keeping up his video calls with Bella.

Alex had told her Matteo had never returned to the yacht from Dubai and the crew were making their way to Southampton without expecting Matteo to return. Alex promised to contact her when he had more information but all she'd received from him was a text that morning saying:

Forgiveness not permission.

She'd sent a question mark in response but hadn't heard anything since.

She pulled out her phone again. Why wasn't she taking the simplest option and phoning him, or even sending a text? Wouldn't that be better than trying to locate him and possibly force a confrontation in his office?

She scrolled to Matteo's contact details and had her thumb over the call button. Then she put the phone on her coffee table. If she was going to call him, she wanted to rehearse what she was going to say first. She went to search for some pen and paper. Words weren't her strong point and she needed to make sure she got them right. She might only have one shot at this, if she was lucky. He could reject her call. And, if she was going to have to resort to leaving a voicemail, she didn't want it to be a rambling, incoherent mess.

Half an hour later, crumpled pieces of paper with her failed attempts were everywhere. This was the reason people went digital. Why was writing from her heart so hard?

She was grateful for the ring of her doorbell—she needed a break to refocus.

When she opened the door, she blinked a few times to make sure she wasn't imagining Matteo standing in front of her.

She sighed. Had her memory downplayed how attractive he was or had he got even more gorgeous in the few weeks they'd been apart?

She stood back to allow him into her flat. Behind his back, she pinched the skin on her wrist—the pain was enough to convince her she wasn't dreaming.

'How did you know where I live?' she asked, her mind blank of anything else as she led him into her living room and gestured for him to sit down.

'Alex gave me your address.'

'Alex?' She furrowed her brow. 'Oh, that explains his text.'

'Pardon?'

She shook her head. 'Nothing. Why are you here, Matteo?'

She'd wanted to see him and been planning out what she had to say to him. But now he was here, in her home in front of her, she felt completely unprepared.

Matteo pulled a piece of paper out of his jacket. 'I have a list of people you can contact who may be able to help you with your job hunt. I can make the introductions if you need.'

A pang in her chest made it feel as if her heart was breaking. He was offering her exactly what he had suspected she had schemed to use him for. She didn't know why he was offering this now, but it didn't really matter. His offer could only mean one thing—he still didn't believe her. He still didn't trust her. The little kernel of hope that had stubbornly refused to die out over the last couple of weeks finally crumbled. And it hurt.

She took a deep breath and blinked to relieve the pressure of the tears building in her eyes.

'Thank you, Matteo. But that's not necessary. I actually have a new job starting soon. I promise you, I didn't work on the yacht to sign you as a client. I can't think of anything I can say to convince you.'

Matteo furrowed his brows. 'I don't think you were using me for your career.'

'What?' she asked, her mouth falling open.

'Okay, my immediate reaction was that you wanted to use me to help me with your career. But it didn't take long to realise I was wrong.'

'You were wrong?' Was she really hearing this?

'Very wrong. The most wrong I've ever been.' He said it with such a matter-of-fact tone, she giggled. He'd admitted he'd been wrong, so did that mean he was ready to trust her?'

'I was looking for a reason to distrust you,' he continued. 'You could have told me you were arrested for releasing the penguins at the zoo and I would have found a way to turn that into a betrayal of me.'

As Deepti crinkled her face, trying to understand his random example, Matteo reached out a finger to trace the furrows on her brow. She grabbed his hand and held it in hers. She never wanted to let go.

'I never cared about what happened with your job,' he said. 'I only cared that you hid it from me. I don't understand why you had to keep it a secret.'

'Neither do I,' Deepti replied with a grimace. 'I didn't trust myself, so nothing I was doing made any sense. I was so sure something I'd done had led to my firing. I was scared of making another mistake or trusting in the wrong people. I was so frightened of making the wrong decision, it made me incapable of making any rational decision at all. You were one of the few good things happening to me and I couldn't risk losing that.'

'I'm sorry I made you feel vulnerable. If I had shown you I trusted you, perhaps you would have been more open with me.'

'You can't blame yourself, Matteo. It was nothing you did. I love you and I just couldn't bear the idea of you thinking badly of me.'

'You love me?'

Deepti automatically covered her mouth, as if that would take back the words that had slipped out. Then she straightened her shoulders.

'This isn't the way I planned to tell you, but yes, I do. I love you. I know we've only known each other for a few weeks, and we barely know each other really, but I have absolutely no doubts about the way I feel about you. I love you.'

Silence greeted her. She could read his look of disbelief, so she continued, 'Please don't feel awkward. I'm not expecting anything—'

'I love you too.'

Deepti's breath came out in a laugh. 'What?'

'I love you, Deepti.'

She threw back her head and laughed with sheer exhilaration. Was this what complete happiness felt like? Giving a small shriek, she threw her arms around him and raised her mouth to meet his…

* * *

A long time later, Matteo leaned against the back of the couch while Deepti went to get some refreshments.

He looked around her living room. It was bright and cosy and perfectly like her. She was a little bit messier than he'd expected, judging by all the crumpled paper on the floor. He noticed a pad of the same type of paper on the coffee table in front of him and leaned forward to take a closer look.

*Hi, Matteo,*
*It's Deepti... Deepti Roy*

It read like a conversation rather than a letter. He laughed. As if he needed her surname, or even her first name! He would have known who it was the moment she spoke.

*I'm sorry for not telling you the truth sooner. I have no excuses. I just wanted to let you know I love you.*

The last three words were circled with an annotation:

*Too soon. Move to nearer the end.*

He smiled up at Deepti when she came back into the room.

'What is this?' he asked.

She squealed and almost spilled the drinks in her rush to place them on the table, before attempting to get the paper out of his hands. She landed on his chest. He dropped the paper, grabbed her closer and covered her with his kisses.

'I adore you,' he said when they finally broke apart.

'I still can't believe it,' she said with a slight shake of her head.

'I'll show you how much every day for the rest of my life, so you never have to doubt it. I never believed in love at first sight until you.'

She sighed deeply. In a quiet, uncertain voice, she asked, 'Are you sure?'

He cupped her face and, staring deep into her eyes, he answered simply, 'Yes.'

'I'm scared, Matteo. We've known each other for such a short time. Barely a month. And our actual relationship was only a few days. I know the way I feel about you is real. I know I truly love you. I want to trust this can last, but I'm scared.'

'I'm scared too. There are no guarantees in this life, but losing Luca suddenly made me realise we have to go after what we want while we still can. And I want you. I know I will always love you. I want you to believe that. I want you to trust that your love for me isn't fleeting and you will always love me too.'

'I really want to. I'm trying to. But I've never felt this way before.'

'Isn't that a reason to believe this time it's different? If we're not meant for each other, why would we feel this strongly?'

She inclined her head. 'You're right. This is the real thing.'

'Then marry me.'

'What?' Her mouth fell open. Her shocked look was so incredibly endearing, he gathered her too him and covered her in long, deep, passionate kisses until they were both out of breath.

When they broke for oxygen, she pushed him away slightly. 'Matteo, you can't just say things like that and then kiss me so I can't think straight.'

He laughed. That sounded perfect to him. He didn't want her to think straight when she was around him. When she was thinking straight, it seemed as though her brilliant, logical mind came up with every possible obstacle to their relationship.

'I'm not asking you to marry me because I want to ease your mind. I'm asking you to marry me because I love you. And I am absolutely certain I want to spend the rest of my life with you.'

Getting off the sofa, he reached into his pocket and pulled out a small jewellery box as he went down on one knee. 'This isn't a whim. You know I don't do things on a whim.' He noticed her grin and qualified his statement. 'Okay, perhaps when it comes to you it feels like I'm making and changing plans on a whim. But you have to understand, I am completely in love with you. I have been from the first moment we met.'

She tilted her head, as if she wasn't sure whether she was hearing him properly or whether he was going to tell her he was joking. He swallowed heavily. She had to believe him. This was the most important answer he had ever waited for. He held his breath.

With a shake of her head, she said, 'I can't believe I'm doing this,' as she held out her hand for the ring.

'That sounds like a yes. Is that a yes?'

She laughed, and then nodded vigorously. 'It's a yes,' she said as she threw herself onto him, her momentum knocking him back onto the floor.

Deepti sat in Matteo's warm embrace, staring at the diamond on her finger. Her family and friends would probably think she was acting out of character but, in the end, accepting Matteo's proposal had been the easiest, most sensible decision she'd ever made.

But there were a lot of decisions still to be

made. They wouldn't sort out everything that day, but they needed to make a start.

'Where do you want to live?' she asked. With Matteo's business interests, they could be facing a long-distance relationship, and she wanted to be prepared.

'Well,' Matteo said, placing a kiss on the top of her head. 'I recently proved I can work from anywhere. The middle of the ocean, if necessary. I suggest the simplest solution is for me to follow you. Where is your new job?'

'London.'

'Then we'll find a place together. Until then, I can move in here, or you can move in with me. If we're going to get married soon, there's no reason not to live together straight away.'

Deepti pulled away slightly and craned her neck to look at him. 'Soon?'

He shrugged. 'Why wait? Unless you want to organise a very big wedding?'

'Not really. To be honest, I never thought about getting married. I never met anyone I felt that strongly about.'

'Until me,' Matteo prompted.

She giggled. 'Until you.'

'Do you want to get married in England or in India?'

She thought about it for a moment. 'Actually,

I think, if we're going to get married soon, I'd like to get married in Singapore.'

'Singapore? So Bella can be there?'

'She is the reason we met.'

'I think serendipity's the reason we met.'

Deepti laughed again. She didn't know if he was referring to his yacht, but he was right. It was through serendipity that she'd met Matteo and it was her destiny to love him, and be loved by him, for ever.

\* \* \* \* \*

*If you enjoyed this story,
check out these other great reads
from Ruby Basu*

Cinderella's Forbidden Prince
Baby Surprise for the Millionaire

*All available now!*